DYING
in the
DARK

ONE WORLD
BALLANTINE BOOKS
NEW YORK

DYING
in the
DARK

VALERIE
WILSON
WESLEY

A TAMARA HAYLE MYSTERY

A One World Book
Published by The Random House Publishing Group

Copyright © 2004 by Valerie Wilson Wesley

www.ballantinebooks.com/one/

Library of Congress Cataloging-in-Publication Data
Wesley, Valerie Wilson.
    Dying in the dark : a Tamara Hayle mystery /
by Valerie Wilson Wesley.
        p.   cm.
    ISBN 0-345-46806-6
    1. Hayle, Tamara (Fictitious character)—Fiction.
2. Women private investigators—New Jersey—
Newark—Fiction.   3. African American women—
Fiction.   4. Female friendship—Fiction.   5. Mothers
and sons—Fiction.   6. Newark (N.J.)—Fiction.
I. Title.
PS3573.E8148D95 2004
813'.54—dc22   2004050089

Manufactured in the United States of America

First Edition: October 2004

9 8 7 6 5 4 3 2 1

Book design by Barbara M. Bachman

FOR MY COUSINS

JANIS SPURLOCK-McLENDON

AND KARLA SPURLOCK-EVANS,

WHO HAVE ALWAYS BEEN

MY SISTERS

John Henry with his hammer

Makes a little spark

That little spark is love

Dying in the dark

—LANGSTON HUGHES

A C K N O W L E D G M E N T S

There are many family members and friends who have always
supported me. My thanks to you all. I'd particularly like to thank my
literary agent Faith Hampton Childs for her wisdom and kindness,
and my editor Melody Guy for her fine editing skills. I'm also
grateful to Regina Waynes Joseph, Esq., Mary Jane Fine, and Valarie
Daniels for their thoughtful "first reads," and to Booker Theodore
Evans, M.D., for his good advice. As always, Richard, Nandi, and
Thembi have my gratitude and abiding love.

DYING
in the
DARK

"Don't never *talk to haints,*" my grandma used to tell me. "Haints" are what the old folks call ghosts, and when she'd say it, my daddy would roll his eyes and shake his head. But I knew what she was talking about. "If one comes knocking at your door, you just turn your head, look in the other direction, and *never* listen to what it has to say." My grandmother has been dead since I was a kid, but her words still rang true even though Celia Jones wasn't an ordinary "haint." She wore green eye shadow, too much rouge, and enough Tabu cologne to make a preacher forget his calling, and the door she knocked on wasn't the kind you walked through. She started showing up in my dreams about a month after she'd been murdered. For three nights straight.

Celia was the closest thing I had to a sister after Pet, my real one, pulled up stakes and split. The two of us would run the streets like wild things: sneaking out, bumming cigarettes and joints, sharing everything from drawers to dudes. We talked smart to men we had no business knowing and hung out places we had no business going. But I had my brother Johnny, may his soul rest in peace, to cool my heels and keep me out of trouble. He was always there when I needed him, even before he became a cop. After that, he'd warn any hardheaded Negro who looked my way to keep his eyes—and hands—off his baby sister.

Celia wasn't so lucky. Her mama was dead, her papa didn't give a damn, and her brothers and sisters were so glad to get out their daddy's house, they steered clear of anything or anybody who reminded them where they came from. Celia was on her own, kicking ass and taking names all by herself. I loved her like she was kin because she was strong, smart, and knew her way around.

Over the years, I hadn't thought too much about her until I saw the headline in the *Star-Ledger*: "Woman Shot, Killer Unknown." It was the kind of story that caught my attention, since I make my living finding out who has done what to whom, and when I saw her name, I lost my breath. Celia had been shot full of holes on New Year's Day in her ground-floor apartment in a dilapidated building off South Orange Avenue. I knew the place, and it made me sad to know she'd ended up there. She was identified as a waitress in a bar on Bergen, the kind of low-life dive you think twice about walking past in broad daylight. There were no suspects, the newspaper said, and no leads. And there were no follow-up stories. I looked every day.

I can't say I shed any tears when I read it. We had known each other a long time ago and not parted as friends. We fought over a man, the dumbest thing in the world two women can fight over, so she'd gone her way and I'd gone mine. The last time I saw her, she was climbing into the driver's seat of a midnight blue Lincoln. She had a Virginia Slims cigarette dangling out her mouth and a men's

T-shirt covering her high pregnant belly. I called her name, and when she turned in my direction, I saw a bruise the size of a silver dollar on the left side of her mouth. She looked straight through me. When we were kids, she used to say she'd kill any man who laid a hand on her, so I couldn't believe what was on her face. I called her again and ran toward the car, and she pulled away from the curb so fast I had to jump out the way to keep from being hit.

"The hell with you, too, Celia Jones!" I screamed into the dust she left and that was that. In that instant I decided I didn't want any part of any trouble she'd gotten herself into. My brother was dead, and I'd just married DeWayne Curtis, my son's father. I was still young enough to think "true love" solved everything, and that that was what I had with DeWayne. I sure didn't want somebody's sorrow shadowing the happiness I'd found. So I let her and her pregnant self go wherever the hell she was going.

Maybe we still had unfinished "girlfriend" business. Maybe I should have searched for her, gone back to some of our spots, found a way to help her. Maybe that was why she came back to haunt me. But, then again, it could have been those ribs I'd bought at Costco's and wolfed down like a fool two nights in a row. Pork will do that to you, if you've sworn it off like I had. Or maybe it was just seeing her name like I had in the paper and wondering who had taken her life so cruelly. It's hard to say what brought Celia back, but I was pretty sure why she'd come.

The dream always started the same. I didn't see her at first. All I saw were hands, calloused and ugly, squeezing deep into the hollow of her slender, brown throat. Her fingernails, with the bright red polish she always wore, were digging into the hands, trying hard to pull them from around her neck. Then I saw the locket I gave her when we graduated from high school. We bought lockets for each other the same day at Bamberger's, the big department store that used to take up half of Market Street but that moved to the suburban malls in the early eighties. The one Celia gave me had a sapphire in the middle, cut glass no doubt. God knows what became of it. The one I gave her had a "ruby" because it was red, her favorite color. We'd both inscribed them with "From your best friend" on the top. In my dream, her locket was pulled tight around her neck, slashing her skin as her body arched. I could feel her choking, fighting for breath, for her life. That was when she looked at me, her green-shadowed eyes bright with fear, her shiny red mouth wide open. I could smell the Tabu.

"Help me!" she said.

I'd wake up then in a sweat, glad to be out of that place and in the safety of my own bedroom.

The first night I dreamed it, I jumped out of bed and ran to my son's room to check on him. The second night, I went downstairs and made myself a pot of Sleepytime tea, then drifted off to sleep on the couch. The third night, I downed two shots of bourbon and wondered why the hell the girl was picking on me. Dreams are nothing but dreams, I reminded myself.

Or so they say.

Then they stopped, and after a night or two, I didn't think about her anymore. After two weeks, I'd forgotten about the dreams altogether. I had other things on my mind, and on the top of my list was buying myself a new car. My dependable blue Jetta, aka the Blue Demon, may she rest in peace, had met a tragic end in a parking lot in Atlantic City, so I was taking cabs and public transportation until I could find a good deal on another one.

So when the kid knocked on my door that Monday morning, I was sitting at my desk, sipping coffee, and going through the used-car ads in the *Star-Ledger.* He came in before I could open it, slumping down in the chair in front of my desk like he had an appointment. It only took a minute to recognize him; his cheekbones and pretty slanted eyes were straight out of his mama.

"You Tamara Hayle?" He had a growl of a voice, too grown for such a skinny kid.

"You're Celia's boy, aren't you?" He nodded and the shy little grin his mama used to pull when she needed to charm somebody spread out on his chapped lips. He was older than my son Jamal, but not by much. I knew he must be that baby she'd been carrying when I last saw her. He was dressed like a gangsta: loose, sloppy pants, bulky sweater, polished Timberland boots, a rolled-back stocking pulled over his soft wavy hair. Celia's hair. A square-cut diamond ring in a platinum setting glittered on his right hand, which was far too big for his delicate fingers.

"Did you hear about my mama?"

"Yes. I'm so sorry. Do they know—"

The rage that came into his face was so intense it made me stop midsentence. Then his eyes watered so quickly I was sure he was going to cry, but he was too big for that. He balled his right hand into a fist and hit the palm of his left hand three times. If he hadn't been a kid, I would have been scared of him. His eyes got hard, and he stared straight out my dirty office window to the buildings outside. When he shifted his gaze back to me, tears were still in his eyes, but he didn't try to keep them back this time. My first impulse was to offer some comfort, but knowing teenage boys like I do, I knew that was the last thing he would want from somebody else's mama. So I sat back and watched them roll down his hollow cheeks straight down to his just-grown beard.

"What's your name?" I asked him.

"Cecil Jones." He raised his chin in an odd show of defiance.

"Cecil Jones," I repeated his name, wondering about the father whose name he didn't carry. "What can I do for you today?" I asked, but I knew what he wanted and that there wasn't a damn thing I could do for him.

"I want you to find out who killed my mama." There it was anyway.

"What have the police told you?" I asked the predictable question.

"Fuck the police." He gave the predictable answer, colored with so much anger I was sorry I'd asked.

"What made you come to me?"

"My mama wrote your address down in her book, and it was open to the page with your name on it the day she died."

"Why do you think that I would be able to do more than the police can?" He looked puzzled, then hurt, then he narrowed his eyes.

"How much you want?" he asked.

"It's not about the money, it's—"

"How much you want?" His voice grew louder, more demanding.

"Nothing," I said in exasperation.

"You work for free?" He looked doubtful, suspicious.

"No, I have a sliding scale. I usually charge fifty to seventy-five dollars an hour plus expenses, depending on the job, but I'm not sure if I should take—"

"You knew my mama, right?" His eyes flashed with anger.

"Not for many years," I said gently.

"You knew my mama, right?" He was a boy again, the tears back in his eyes.

"Yeah."

"Why won't you do it then?"

I paused for a moment, running through my options, trying to think of an excuse so I wouldn't have to get involved. It's usually wise to let the past stay in the past. But sometimes I'm not a wise woman, and something inside me told me I didn't have a choice.

"Okay," I said, giving in.

"Then how much you want?"

"Look, you're a kid, so whatever you can manage is fine. If you don't have the money now, I can bill you when you get grown or you can pay me whatever you can pay me." He smiled a quick, confident grin, Celia's grin when she beat me at poker.

"I got money." He pulled an assortment of items out of his pocket: a box cutter, two felt pens, a beeper, a pack of chewing gum, a cell phone, a small plastic case, and a thick wad of bills held together by a rubber band. He peeled off four hundred dollars in twenties, counted them twice, then slammed them down on the desk between us. "That enough?" He shoved the rest of the money and his other things back into his pockets.

"Where did you get all that money?"

"Is that enough to start?"

"Yeah," I said, picking up the money, worrying about where he got it, but knowing that there was no way in hell he would ever tell me. I sighed and put it back down on the table, then decided maybe I owed the kid the benefit of a doubt. "That's enough to start."

"When you going to start then?" he asked with a child's impatience.

"We can start now, if you want to. But first, I need you to answer a few questions, and I want you to be as honest with me as you can, even though the answers might make you uncomfortable. When something like this happens, the smallest thing or answer to an embarrassing question is the very thing that will lead me to where I want to go, do you understand?"

He thought about it for a moment. "Okay."

"I also want you to understand that at some point, I will probably have to involve the police. Are you okay with that?"

A longer pause. "Yeah."

I took out a pad and pencil to jot down some notes.

"Do you have any idea why your mother wrote my name in her book?"

"Naw, all she wrote was Tamara Hayle, Hayle Investigative Services. I found the book in her room when I found her."

A chill went through me as I put my pen down. "You found your mother's body?"

"Yeah." He spoke with no emotion, and I knew that he wasn't able to feel it yet, and it would be a long time before he'd be able to, if he ever did. It had been taken me a decade to get over finding my brother, and I am still haunted by it. Some things never leave you.

"Was she afraid of anybody?"

A shadow crossed his face, and I knew without pushing it that she was, so I didn't wait for an answer. "When did this person threaten her?"

His face turned to stone, and I could see that however tough this kid thought he was, his mama had been dealing with somebody bigger and badder, and he might still be scared of whoever it was.

"So you're not sure who was threatening her?"

"No."

"Do you know why she didn't go to the police?"

"She did. She went a couple of times." His voice cracked.

"So they didn't do anything?"

"Naw. They didn't do shit."

I made a quick note to check with the cops about restraining orders placed by Celia against boyfriends, past or present.

"Was she dating anybody?"

The sound that came out of his mouth was somewhere between a grunt and a laugh. "Dating? My mama?"

I put it bluntly. "Did your mother have a man?"

He sighed, an old man's sigh. "There was always dudes hanging around my mama," he said. That had always been the case with Celia Jones. She was never without a man for long, not even as a teenager. Traveling with a pair and a spare she used to call it.

"What about your father?" His eyes widened, but I couldn't tell what emotion was behind them. "Do you have any contact with him?"

He studied me for a long time before he answered me. "Yeah. Every now and then, my old man comes by."

"And his name is?"

He paused for so long I wondered if he knew it. "Brent. That's who my daddy is. Brent Liston."

I tried to conceal my reaction, but couldn't quite do it. I'd known Brent Liston in high school. He was the first of the "bad" boys Celia hung out with who actually ended up doing time in prison. He hadn't been a bad kid then, but a troubled one with a temper that could turn mean at the drop of a dime. But he had been good-looking and charming in his own rough way. He'd ended up doing time in Rahway for shooting his cousin over a hundred bucks in a drunken game of blackjack. I'd heard he was out. I wondered if the kid knew his father's history.

"Have you seen your father recently?"

He didn't say anything.

"Had your mother?"

He shrugged.

"Do you know if they ever had a violent confrontation?" The way the kid's face dropped told me that my question had come out of left field. I knew the murder had probably been committed by somebody Celia knew well, and a man who had just done some years for killing somebody over a card game was as likely a suspect as any. I wondered if the cops had talked to him yet.

"No. He never hit her."

I waited a couple of beats before I asked the next one.

"Do you think he could have done this to your mama?"

"No. I know he definitely didn't do it. I know that! He wouldn't do nothing like that!"

I didn't push it. That would come later.

"Who was she afraid of, Cecil?" He glanced down at his hands, not wanting to answer, so I asked again.

"I don't know the names, I told you, dudes were always hanging around her."

"And you don't know which one was threatening her?"

"No."

"But it wasn't your father?" I went back to Brent Liston.

"I told you already. Naw, it wasn't my father." I thought about Jamal and his relationship with my ex-husband, DeWayne Curtis. Jamal could talk about his father like a dog, but if he heard anybody utter the slightest criticism, he was on them like white on rice. No matter what DeWayne did, he was still his father, and that counted for something.

"About the book you got my name from? Do you still have it?" There might be names I could follow up with, even Brent Liston's number or address.

He pulled a book covered in red cloth out of an inside pocket and put it on my desk. I picked it up, glanced through it, then put it back down. "I'd like to keep it, okay?"

"It was my mama's."

"It will only be for a couple of days while I go through it, and then I'll give it back."

He looked doubtful. "Okay."

His beeper went off, and he pulled it out, glanced at me, then at the beeper, then pulled out his cell phone, changed his mind about using it, and put it back in his pocket.

"Can we talk later on? I got an appointment." He looked nervous, and I wondered exactly what kind of business this boy was in.

"Sure." I pulled out my appointment book. "What about tomorrow, around this time."

"Okay."

"By the way, where do you live?"

"Sometimes I stay with my girlfriend over on Eighteenth Street. But you can reach me at one of these numbers if you need to talk to me." He jotted down three numbers on the edge of the blotter on my desk. I stood up to shake his hand. He looked surprised, but when I smiled he returned it. Celia's smile.

"I'll ask around, see what I can find out. But don't get your hopes up. I'm sure the cops are still trying to find out who killed your mother, and I really think you should talk to them again."

"I'll think about it," he said.

"Everything will be okay, Cecil." He nodded like he believed me.

After he left, I put his money and the book into a safe I had recently installed. It was then that I noticed the small case he'd left on the edge of my desk. I wasn't surprised when I opened it to find Celia's locket. The fact that she'd kept it for all these years brought tears to my eyes. I placed it in the safe with the money and the book, planning to give it back to Cecil when I saw him the next day.

But the next day came and went, as did the next, and when I hadn't heard from him by Thursday, I called the first number he'd jotted down on the blotter.

"What you want with him?" The woman's voice was rough and ugly.

"Who is this?" I asked her.

"What you want with him?"

"Just let me talk to him, please."

The woman choked out a laugh that sounded like a croak and came from the back of her throat. "You better make yourself a date with St. Peter then. That boy was stabbed through his heart Monday night. He dead and gone, just like his slut of a mama," she said.

CHAPTER TWO

I don't remember hanging up the phone or even what I was thinking. I just felt cold, as if somebody had shoved a bag of ice into the center of my heart. By the time I got myself together enough to ask the woman for more information, the line was dead. When I called back, the phone was either busy or off the hook; I suspected the latter. So all I knew for sure was that the kid was dead, that he had left my office and run into somebody evil who had wiped him, the last little bit of Celia Jones, off this earth. I've seen a lot of death in my time: my parents, my brother Johnny, more good folks than bad. But when a kid dies like this one did, his future gone before he knew he had one, it's hard as hell for me to shake it off. I'm used to death, but I ain't that used to it.

I'd never seen so much sorrow in a kid's eyes, and the thought of it made me utter one of those long, sad sighs that take everything out of you. I finally got up to make myself some tea, hoping it would make me feel better. Celestial Seasonings is my brand, and I picked through the assortment I keep in a plastic bag in my desk drawer for something to soothe my nerves. Sleepytime wasn't going to do it.

Red Zinger had too much zing. I settled on Tension Tamer, then laughed out loud at my choice. Hell, there wasn't that much "tension tamer" in the world. A slug of bourbon from that bottle Wyvetta Green, the owner of Jan's Beauty Biscuit, keeps stashed in her closet would do me better, and I thought about going downstairs to ask her for a shot.

But it was very late on a Friday night, and although Wyvetta worked late on Fridays, she was probably on her way out. She was a good friend, and I knew she'd help me out if she could, but there wasn't anything she or anyone else could do about what had happened. The boy was dead. His mama was dead, and as far as I knew, I was their last and only link to the living.

I won't lie about it. Part of me wanted to forget the whole damn thing. I didn't really know the boy, I reminded myself. He'd shown up with his bad-boy attitude topped with his mama's smile and forced his woeful little self into my world. As for Celia Jones, that was one sister who was decidedly in my past. And what *was* that dream about anyway? Leftover thoughts from some article in the *Ledger*? My belly turned sour on ribs gobbled down in record-breaking time? It was plain foolish of me to think that a woman, dead as she was, could send me messages from her grave. Yet I could still hear her voice.

Help me!

"'To hell with you, Celia Jones!" I said aloud what I'd once before declared through the dust of that car. I had too many other things on my mind now to worry about Celia and her wayward child. I had my own son to take care of, a car to buy, and half-dozen unpaid bills stashed in the top drawer of my desk. True, things weren't as bad as they sometimes are. Although my life is usually a struggle between broke and broker, this year hadn't been half bad. But I wasn't rich enough to spend time looking for a killer who even the cops had probably given up on finding. Time is money in my business. I charge by the hour, and I've got to be smart about how I use my time. I'd bet the bucks I owe PSE&G, my unforgiving utility company, that the police already had a lead on the bastard who stabbed Celia's boy, and that would probably lead to who had killed her. They sure as hell had more resources than me. Maybe for once, I should leave it to the experts. Truth was, Celia and Cecil Jones had confronted someone hateful and vicious enough to kill them both, and I sure didn't want that craziness touching me or my child.

But talk between my head and my heart are two different conversations, and my heart told me I'd gotten involved in Celia's mess the moment her child walked through my door. He had plopped down his $400 in good faith. I owed it to my client, dead as he was, to do what was right. I didn't have a choice.

So I plugged in my electric kettle and while I waited for the whistle, started looking through my tea bag collection for something with caffeine; later for taming my tension. Lipton does the job in a pinch if I spike it with a load of sugar, so I dropped four tea bags into the black flowered teapot, which Jamal had given me for my birthday, poured in some water, and brewed myself a cup of tea strong and sweet enough to pull me out of my funk.

After a few sips, I turned on my old-ass, no-name computer and waited for it to boot up. A couple of years back, I finally saved enough money to buy a new one, and ended up giving it to Jamal, who needed it more than me. My attitude toward my computer is like my attitude used to be toward the Blue Demon; it would have to do me until its last gasp. It was also a comforting thought that if some nosy somebody broke into my office one night and tried to pull up a file, he'd still be sitting here when I walked in the next morning.

When the thing finally lit up, I typed a date on the screen, saved the file as "redlocket," and typed in the facts I knew about Celia and Cecil Jones and the details of my meeting with the boy. I searched through my file cabinet for the *Star-Ledger* article about Celia's murder and found it tucked under a stack of old Macy's bills. I shook my head at my own self-deception when I read it.

Whenever I thought about Celia's murder, I imagined it happening as it had in my dream—her eyes big with terror, her red nails clawing somebody's hands. But she had been killed by multiple gunshot wounds from a .22 caliber weapon. Popular wisdom says the .22 is a woman's gun, a lady's little protector that fits neatly into a purse or handbag. But I know from experience that a .22 is as lethal and quick as a .38, if you aim it right and shoot at close range. My guess was that Celia's killer had pumped half a dozen bullets into her, pleased with the thought that he was bound to strike something vital. When somebody kills like that, he wants it to hurt; there's hatred in every shot.

I wondered if the cops had made any progress on her case. Most cops are reluctant to share information on a murder still under investigation, and officially they'd still be looking into Celia's, even though it was more than a month old. But her son's killing would be the one they'd really be interested in because it was fresh. I typed down a note to myself to ask my friend Jake if he'd heard anything about the progress on that one. Not that I needed to remind myself. Despite what is, what isn't, and what I wish were between us, Jake Richards is my first, last, and most important resource.

I took from the safe the red book and plastic case the boy had left and brought them to my desk. The case was a cheap, tacky number Celia had probably picked up for a buck and a half in one of those 99-cent bargain stores. I'd done my share of shopping in places like that, and was sure that Celia had, too. The book, which was the size of a diary, was more expensive. Upon close examination, I saw that it was covered with red cloth made up of tiny hearts, which made me smile. Celia was born on Valentine's Day, and even Christmas had taken second place in her hierarchy of favorite holidays. She had always had a sentimental side to her, crying at sad movies, buying food for some poor, bedraggled cat, remembering your birthday when everybody else forgot it. She didn't let a lot of folks see that tender part of her; hard times and harder men taught her to cover it up, but I knew it was there, and I was sure her son did, too. Did her murderer know it?

The book was brand new, the pages still crisp and white. The price tag on the back cover was legible, and I could see that the original price had been cut by half, which suggested that it may have been part of some post-Christmas sale. The boy had been right about my name. It was the first thing I saw when I opened it. She'd printed it along with my address and telephone number in big, bold letters like a kid does, forming each one carefully, as if she were afraid of getting something wrong.

Her boy had said that the book had been opened to my name when he found her. When did she plan to call me? I wondered. If she'd bought the book after Christmas, calling me may have been part of some New Year's Day resolution. People sometimes reach out to old friends on the first of the year. It's a time to renew acquaintances, make amends, apologize for past wrongs. She'd written "Hayle Investigative Services" next to my name, which suggested that maybe she wanted to use my professional services; the boy had said as much when he came to see me.

But maybe I was wrong about the timing. There was no way to know what her intentions were. The only thing I knew for sure was that she'd been murdered on New Year's Day. Had she spent New Year's Eve with her killer? Could her death have been somebody's New Year's resolution?

On the top of the next page, she printed the letters ABCD, encircling them with hearts and arrows. It was the kind of scribbling a teenager does when she has nothing much on her mind. I couldn't tell whether the hearts and arrows were connected to a particular letter or if they were simply put down randomly. Had she been jotting down the alphabet for the hell of it? Or could the letters stand for names, the "B" for the "B" in Brent, the "C" for Celia or Cecil? Chances were that the whole thing meant squat, but I typed the letters on my screen anyway—A, B, C, D—with "Brent Liston" who only showed up "every now and then" according to the kid, in parentheses behind the "B."

The pages that followed were filled with scraps of indecipherable scribbles, what seemed to be lists of gifts for her son, lines of poetry, and the titles of self-help books. I finally struck gold on the last page. Halfway down, she'd scribbled three names and numbers in red ink. I typed the names and the matching numbers onto my screen, then called each of them.

The first belonged to someone named Rebecca Donovan. The phone rang four times before it was answered by a woman with a pretentious British accent who told me in a no-nonsense voice that I'd reached Ms. Donovan's answering service and that Ms. Donovan, with an emphasis on the Ms., would return my call on Monday. Although the woman didn't say exactly what Rebecca Donovan did, I assumed she had some kind of a professional relationship with Celia, probably in a "helping" capacity. I knew from my experience with Karen, the hardworking sister whose twenty-four-hour answering service I use, that you don't bother with a service unless you need to get your calls screened. When you run a business like mine, you never know when some nut is going to get your number from the yellow pages and call you with foolishness you don't want to be bothered with. I was sure that Ms. Donovan, whoever she was, paid plenty for that clipped British accent. Karen, with her home-girl attitude and occasional lapses in judgment and grammar, came cheap. I love the sister, but for a hot minute, I wondered how Hayle Investigative Services would sound in that high-class professional voice. That would be one way to let losers know that *Ms.* Tamara Hayle was definitely beyond *their* reach.

A sullen teenager answered the phone for Annette Sampson, the second number on the page. I left my name and number, but knew from experience with my occasionally sullen teenage son that she probably wouldn't get it until sometime next week. I made a note to call her back on Monday morning.

Aaron Dawson, the owner of the last number, apparently wasn't at home either, or at least wasn't answering his phone. I tried him again, then gave up. On impulse, I called the three numbers the kid had jotted down on my blotter, with no responses. I couldn't forget the undisguised contempt for both Celia and Cecil that had been in that woman's voice, and whoever she was, she didn't answer again. I added those numbers to the screen, saved the file, and decided to call it a night. It was time for me to go home and spend some time with my son.

I'd almost forgotten about the plastic case next to the book. Before I put it away, I opened it, took out the locket, and read the inscription: ". . . best friend."

Within a month, we'd both forgotten about the fool who had torn us apart, and all that remained was our anger. But she had been my best friend on that warm June day, when loving each other like sisters, we'd bought and exchanged our gifts.

"Catch you later, girl," I whispered, uttering the farewell we always said when we parted, and the long-gone teenage girl I'd once been was back in my voice. We'd believed then that we could beat anything the world threw our way and that nothing could change how we felt about each other. Tears welled in my eyes for the loss of her life and my innocence. The locket was mine now, back with the "best friend" who had bought it.

A cold gust of wind blew in from somewhere, startling me. Impulsively, I glanced at the locket and then at the window, which I saw was cracked. I chuckled at my uneasiness. It was wind from the open window, not Celia's spirit, that had sent me shivering. I'd had enough haunting by my old friend for one day. But difficult friends, even dead ones, can be hard to shake.

I put the necklace back into the safe along with the book, then filled a glass with water to pour on the orphan aloe plant that had taken up residence in a corner of my window. I called my aloe an orphan because years ago I found it, dusty and stunted, on my doorstep. Nobody—not Annie, my best friend who owns the building, nor Wyvetta from downstairs—claimed to have put it there, so I became its adopted mama. My orphan aloe had aged like me and everything else in my life. I smiled tenderly down at it as I poured water into its roots.

It was then that I saw him.

He was dressed in a black, heavy coat that fell to his ankles. I couldn't see his face, but I knew that the light from my office made it easy for him to see mine. He stared up toward my window, as if spellbound by what he saw. He made no movement, no nod of his head or shift of his arms or legs. He just stood there staring up, and it felt like a violation of my space and of me. I pulled back into the shadows even though I knew it was too late.

What did he want with me? Was it simply chance that he was standing here under my window tonight? Instinct, which I have in spades, told me that chance had nothing to do with it, that he wanted something only I could give him. Fear squeezed my stomach tight, and for a moment I couldn't catch my breath.

"No," I said aloud, speaking to the fear as if it were a person. "You're not going to get me! You're not going to take me over! Why the hell should I be scared of you?" I spoke to the man. "Who the hell do you think you are, trying to scare me like this? Fuck you, you dumb bastard!"

It felt good to say it, real good, and I jerked down the shade, nearly pulling it off the roller as I cut him from my view. But even as

I did it, I knew I would see him again. I had to leave my office and leave the building. I had to walk five long blocks to catch the bus and another three and half from the bus stop to my house. I drew in my breath, pulled the shade up again, and searched for him in the darkness. But he was gone.

CHAPTER THREE

I *was uneasy as I waited* for the bus and then walked from the bus stop to my home. My house was dark when I entered it. I stood in the kitchen frozen with fear before I found the light, snapped it on, and as calmly as I could, yelled out for my son. That was when I saw the Post-it on the refrigerator explaining that he'd gone to the movies with a "friend" (didn't mention the gender), and he'd be back before one. My apprehension dissolved into annoyance, but I relaxed.

Things sure had changed. In the old days, I could count on Jamal being here when I got home from work. Sometimes he'd have some makeshift little meal, usually out of a can, waiting for me. Often he would simply be doing his homework with the TV on for company and greet me with a grin that reminded me why I got up every morning to meet the madness.

My boy is growing up. He'll be heading to college in a few years, and I'm swept by loneliness whenever I think about it. I dread being alone in this house, filled as it is with memories. Part of me doesn't want Jamal to go. I know that's selfish as hell, but it's the truth, and I've reached the point in my life where I can't lie to myself about anything. But the reality of motherhood is that you raise a child to let him go or you both end up crippled. Learning to be alone is a skill I'll need to master; I don't have a choice.

I felt sorry for myself for a minute or two, then opened a can of black bean soup and made a tuna fish sandwich with a double dose of mayonnaise. I watched a cop show, turned on the news, filled my bathtub with lavender bath oil, and soaked for fifteen minutes. I climbed into bed around eleven-thirty, but I tossed and turned as I listened for the sound of the back door lock that would tell me Jamal was home safely. I couldn't fall asleep until I heard it. He came in sometime after midnight, and I drifted off to sleep. But it was a restless, fitful sleep, and my face must have shown it the next morning. It was the first thing Jamal noticed when he bounced down the stairs for breakfast.

"Hey, Ma, you feeling okay?"

"Yeah, why do you ask?" I knew only too well. My face can't take a sleepless night or too much wine before I go to bed. If I don't get a restful sleep, I look like hell the next morning. "I look that bad, huh? It must be these dark circles and bags that have etched themselves under my eyes." I smiled at his concern.

"No, Ma, you look great!" He gave me a reassuring peck on the cheek. My son has grown tactful with age and understands the vanity of women. "I just thought, well, you looked like maybe you were worried about something."

I took a sip of coffee and turned back to the used-car section of the *Star-Ledger*. "The usual crap, honey. Bills, bills, bills."

I'd decided not to share the details of yesterday's encounter with the man in the black coat. I didn't want to hear about the perils of my profession, which Jamal brings up with alarming regularity, and I certainly didn't want him getting the crazy idea that it was up to him to protect me. He sat down across from me and emptied the contents of the Cheerios box into his bowl.

"My worries include grocery bills, too, kid. How about going easy on that cereal and supplementing it with some toast and a couple of bananas."

"Things are *that* bad?" The smile dropped from his face, which brought one to mine.

"No, I'm just playing with you. Don't worry about it." I was so used to watching every dime, I'd scolded him without thinking about it. Things weren't bad enough yet to deny the boy a bowl of cereal when he wanted it. But Jamal can definitely pack it away, and I remind myself daily that he's a growing boy. He's taller and heavier than I am and obviously takes after his father's side of the family. Thank God, height and weight are the only things he inherited.

"So what you doing today?"

"I was going to catch a game later on with Jake, if that's okay with you."

"Sure." I monitor my expressions whenever Jake Richards's name comes into our conversation, so I kept my eyes glued to the paper. Jake and I are friends, more than anything else, and I've made sure that Jamal understands the limits of our relationship. With the intuition about your love life that only your child possesses, he probably sensed the unspoken, but he knew enough to keep it to himself.

"He's got tickets for the Nets tonight at Continental Arena. If they end up going to the play-offs, Jake said he'll get tickets to that, too. He'll pick me up and drop me off later. So what's going on with the car situation?" he asked in the same breath.

"Sick of the bus, eh?"

"I really miss the Blue Demon."

"So do I." We gave a collective sigh, and then laughed at our mutual grief over the loss of our old Jetta, whose violent demise had saddened us both. The Demon had become a member of our small family—a coughing, raspy, embarrassing member, but kin nevertheless.

"Rayson's Used Cars has a Black History Month sale on. I'm going to take the bus over and see what I can do. Who knows? Maybe I'll pick you up at Jake's tonight in our new car. I'll call and let you know what happens."

"For real?" Excitement shone in his eyes. So much for the Demon's memory.

"Say a little prayer." He clasped his hands, closed his eyes, and for an instant I could see the little boy who once knelt beside his bed at night. I studied the paper to keep him from seeing what was in my eyes.

"Anything good in the *Ledger*?" He gulped down his juice and topped off another glass.

"Not really, but—" I stopped midsentence. A funeral announcement in the Death Notices section had caught my eye. I don't usually read the obituary page; life can be depressing enough without reminding yourself of the Great Beyond, but this one jumped out at me. It was a simple obit. The kid hadn't lived long enough yet to get a full paragraph; a few basic sentences was all he got.

CECIL JONES, 17, FEBRUARY 3, OF NEWARK.

BELOVED SON OF BRENT LISTON OF NEWARK.

FUNERAL SERVICES WILL BE HELD AT 6:00 PM ON SATURDAY,

FEBRUARY 8, AT MORGAN'S FUNERAL HOME, EAST ORANGE.

There was no mention of Celia or how he had died. Beloved son of Brent Liston. That was a laugh.

"What about your father? Do you have any contact with him?"

"Every now and then, my old man comes by."

Disgusted, I slapped the paper down on the table, which, of course, got Jamal's attention. He picked it up and read the section I'd left open.

"Wow! Damn! That's cold! I wonder who took CJ out?"

Red flags popped up. "So you, uh, knew Cecil Jones?"

Jamal shrugged and turned to the sports pages. I took his silence to mean that he did. "And what makes you think somebody took him out, Jamal? The paper doesn't say anything about the way he died. He could have been ill or been hit by a car. Why do you think he was murdered?"

He shrugged again, his defensiveness telling me he didn't want to talk. *Don't ask too many questions, Ma. Don't get too close.* You walk a thin line when you parent a son alone. You know you can't overprotect him, yet you always want to.

"So where do you know him from?" I said, my voice unnaturally calm.

Jamal glanced up at me. "So where do *you* know him from?" The comment was just this side of fresh, and there was a hint of a smile on his lips, but I chose to ignore it. I choose my battles these days, and this one wasn't worth an opening shot. "School," he said after a moment. "I know him from school." He picked up the sports pages again, a defense against more questions.

In the last few years, many good things have happened in Newark and East Orange, the small neighboring city where I live. NJPAC, the arts center that they built a couple of years ago, has changed the mood here forever. Despite naysayers who swore that nothing decent could come out of this city, music, art, and poetry are bringing people back. Property values are rising, carjacking is down, and there's pride in people's voices when they say where they live. There are, of course, still those folks who have their doubts. I took it personally when they tried to change the name of Newark Airport, which it had been for years, to Liberty Airport. People raised so much hell, they ended up calling it Newark Liberty Airport. It's a mouthful, and it still rankles. At least we had the power to raise some hell.

However, there are ominous signs here, too. A few months back, a child's battered body was found in the closet of a filthy basement. His two little brothers, also starved and beaten, had been left for dead. It was a kick in the face of the city, and everybody felt the city's shame. It doesn't say much for a place when children are starved to death and nobody notices. There was a big funeral for the boy, and hundreds of people showed up. Funerals, though, are always for the living, and this one was held to assuage people's guilt. A death like that leaves its mark on a city like mine; it's a reminder that we have a long way to go.

There is also graffiti on walls and abandoned buildings that remind those who know how to read it, that gangs are back—if they ever left. They were around when I was a kid, and for a hot minute, my brother Johnny belonged to one. But weapons have changed, and a "beef" between boys—or girls—can mean a funeral.

I can't afford a private school for my son, and there's no controlling who he comes into contact with in the public school he attends. He's the kind of kid who makes friends easily, and his friends run the gamut. Some like sports and are into computers like he is. They're headed for college and know they have a future. But those are the boys who always seem to end up getting shot over nothing, standing in the way at some rally, strolling down the street on a Saturday night. The good ones always seem to be the ones who end up with a bullet in the back.

There are also kids in Jamal's life who I'd rather he didn't know. He's been friends with some of them since grade school, when they didn't seem too bad. He's always been able to see the good in people, to find gold glimmering in dirt. But that ability, to peer into somebody's soul and see something worth saving, can get you into trouble and for a young black man, trouble will get you dead.

Some nights I can't sleep for worrying about him. Black boys can't make a false move because second chances are hard as hell to come by. I worry about him knowing kids on their way to jail or the graveyard; I don't want him going along for the ride. Even in death, I didn't want Cecil Jones anywhere near my son.

It was time to fire that opening shot.

"So you know Cecil Jones from school? I don't like to hear that, Jamal. Was he one of your friends?" I raised my voice loud enough to show I meant business and to get his attention from behind the paper. He folded it and laid it down on the table.

"CJ didn't go to my school, but he knew guys who do, so he used to hang out there a lot."

"And CJ, as you call him, was a friend of one of your friends?"

He hesitated just a tad too long. "No, Ma, Cecil was not a friend. He was just a dude I knew. Everybody knew him. He hung with a bunch of guys that I definitely try to avoid. So don't worry about me."

"Of course, I worry about you! This kid has been stabbed by who knows what and you know the kids he hung with! Why shouldn't I be worried?"

"So he was stabbed?"

"Yes."

He shook his head sadly and said in a subdued voice, "Ma. Here's the deal. You don't want guys like CJ and his boys thinking *you* think you're better than them, right? So you stay out their way, you watch your back when you're around them, you don't get too tight with them, but you still acknowledge them and stuff. You give them their props and show them you have respect for them. You're cool with them." His face took on a weariness that I'd never seen before, and in that instant I could see him as a grown man, laying down the truth as he knew it to somebody who needed to hear it.

"And you were cool with Cecil Jones?"

"Yeah, I was cool with him. I used to be cool with one of his boys in fifth grade, but not anymore. Now it's just enough to get me by. Like I said, he didn't really go to my school, but he was around. I think he dealt drugs or something."

"Oh God! So you know guys who deal drugs?"

"Ma, what do you think?" He gave me a look that was at the same time helpless and incredulous, reminding me again just how grown he had become.

"And who were his boys?"

He avoided my eyes, and then said after a minute, "This guy named DeeEss, the kid I used to know."

"And don't anymore, right?"

He nodded. "And another one called Pik, dudes like that."

"And they deal drugs, too?"

"I don't know. I told you, I avoid those guys. They probably do. Yeah, they do. Enough of the third degree! I'm not a suspect, okay?" There was a hint of annoyance in his voice that I ignored.

"Do you know his girlfriend?"

"Cristal?" His eyes lit up when he said her name, which, I knew from observing men, wasn't so much recognition as acknowledgment of a certain kind of woman. I started to say something about his attitude, but decided to let it be.

But I did add as innocently as I could, "So her name is Cristal, like the champagne?"

"I guess so, Ma, that's what they call her anyway. I don't know!" He threw up his hands in a dramatic gesture of helplessness and picked up the sports page again, which told me I wasn't going to get anything else out of him.

"Thank you, Jamal."

"For what?"

"For being honest with me."

"You're my mother, I have to be honest with you."

"Have you ever tried drugs?" I asked after a moment, my eyes piercing his.

"No, Ma. Do I act like I do drugs?" He did a half-ass imitation of somebody high on something that made me smile despite myself. "There's no way I'm going to be into drugs living with somebody who's always in my business."

"And you know I'll stay in your business."

"Yeah, how well I know," he said with a smile that told me that despite his attitude he was glad I was. "Now tell me how *you* know Cecil Jones?"

"A case."

"What kind of a case."

"He came to my office."

"Why?"

"He had something he wanted me to do for him."

"What?"

"It doesn't matter now, he's dead."

"Are you going to find out who killed him?"

"I don't know yet."

"Ma, just be careful, okay? Promise me?" he said with so much concern it made me smile because they were exactly the words I always said to him.

After our talk, I decided I'd better make it my business to attend Cecil Jones's funeral later on that day. I was certain his friends—this Pik guy, DeeEss, and Cristal—would show up, and I needed to check them out, for Jamal's sake as well as for my own. But first I had to attend to the "car situation" as Jamal put it. After last night's experience, I had no intention of waiting for a bus. I showered, dressed, and splurged on a cab to Rayson's Used Cars.

CHAPTER FOUR

The day was clear but cold, and I didn't want to spend any more time than absolutely necessary strolling around a used-car lot. Drawn by my fond memories of the Demon, I immediately walked to the section marked pre-used Volkswagens to start my search. Buying a car is a bit like falling in love: You know it when it happens. The Demon's replacement had to be worthy of its predecessor; I knew what I was looking for.

A thin, aggressive man descended on me the moment I walked into the lot. His name tag said "Frank," and his suit, a bright blue number with an odd shine to it, was a size too big. His pug nose seemed a bit too small for his face, and his fingernails were bitten to the quick. With a patronizing grin and one of the worst cases of halitosis I'd ever experienced, he began running down the "virtues" of each of the ugliest cars in the lot. The losers he was pushing couldn't hold the Demon's hubcaps.

"How about a Yugo?" he finally asked, after detailing the "winning points" of the last of the sorry group. "Considering your limited price range—" he stopped midsentence when he saw the expression on my face. My "limited" price range was the very best I could do. The insurance on the Blue Demon hadn't amounted to squat, and I'd had to go into my home equity loan, which I'd taken out to help pay for Jamal's college tuition, to give me the extra edge.

Poor as I was, though, I had my pride. As I tried to come up with a pithy response that would put him in his place, I spotted *the* car, tucked away in a far corner of the lot. It was parked midway between a ten-year-old Volvo and a two-year-old Chevy. It was a newer, sleeker, cherry-red version of the Blue Demon. I was in love.

"How much is that one?" I said to Frank as I pointed toward it in a trance.

More than you've got was written on his face, but he didn't respond to my question.

"How much did you say it was?" I asked him again.

When he told me, I took a deep breath and began calculating what I would need to cut out of my life. No more manicures, pedicures, or trips to the Biscuit; I'd have to depend upon the kindness of Wyvetta Green. No more ribs or apple pies from Costco. No more trips to Red Lobster or Chinese food from the restaurant down the street. McDonald's would be out of my range. Bath oil and foot massage lotion from the Body Shop would be luxuries of the past. Was I really willing to give it all up?

Yet there was something about the way it gleamed in the late morning sun, the windshield sparkling without a chip or nick, the antenna arrow-straight and tall on the hood. The passenger and driver's side windows shining with nary a crack, the door handles unbroken and polished.

"So how about those Yugos?" Frank took his cue from my silence.

Beaten down by reality, I headed with a sigh toward the Yugo section. But then a hand—a strong, sure masculine one—planted itself firmly on my shoulder.

"So what stroke of luck has brought you back into my life?" he said, repeating nearly the same words he'd said to me years before.

And here was my past, slapping me square across my face once again.

Larry Walton wasn't drop-dead gorgeous like Jake Richards. He didn't possess that make-your-panties-wet sensuality that marks Basil Dupre, who can *quickly* make you forget the good sense grandma and *her* mama taught you. But he had a carefree kindness accentuated with an impish dimple in his chin that hinted there was more to him than you saw at first glance. He made you smile even if you felt like crap, which was how I felt the last time I saw him.

I had just left DeWayne Curtis, my fool of an ex-husband, and was discovering how tough it was to raise a kid by myself. My half-ass job as a cop in Belvington Heights was kicking my butt daily, and nightly bouts with Ben & Jerry's Cherry Garcia ice cream had added thirty pounds to my frame. I was a menace to society and to myself. Sorrow seemed to be my lot in life.

It was Thursday night and I was on my way home after a grueling day. I had just picked up a fried whiting sandwich and a side of fries from my favorite fried fish place on Central Avenue and was hugging the greasy bag to my chest like a talisman. In my other hand, I grasped a plastic shopping bag brimming with a six-pack of beer, a box of super tampons, two jumbo bags of Oreos, and a carton of orange juice. I'd tucked the Cherry Garcia into my handbag for safekeeping. I was sweaty, smelly, and unfit for human encounter. The last thing I needed to hear was some tired-ass Negro rap, so when those words tumbled out of his mouth, my eyes ripped through him like razors. But then he smiled with that cute little dimple and suddenly "stroke of luck" didn't sound so corny.

He had always been a fit, good-looking man who wore his clothes like he was headed somewhere special, as he probably was that night. DeWayne Curtis routinely dressed better than me, so I knew an expensive shirt when I saw one. He gave me the kind of hug that makes you feel protected and desirable all at the same time, and told me how good I looked (which I knew was a lie) and how glad he was to see me (which may have been the truth). We talked about nothing for fifteen minutes—what we'd been doing, what we wanted to do. As he turned to leave, we both noticed the greasy stain, courtesy of my fish sandwich bag, left on his shirt. He just laughed about it and said it was worth every greasy inch just to run into me again. He walked me to the Demon, kissed me on the cheek, and watched from the curb as I pulled away. I went home that night with a grin on my face and felt better about myself, life, and everybody in it for the rest of the week. I never forgot it.

The years had treated him well. He'd grown into his looks the way some men do. The dimple was still there, of course, and he was still dressing good. He hugged me for old times' sake, and the hug hadn't changed either. I hoped he didn't remember the fish sandwich.

"I'm here to buy a car," I said.

"And I'm here to sell one. I own this place now. Bought it five years ago from Rayson."

For the next five minutes, he filled me in on the particulars about buying and selling cars. Things had gone well for him, he said, which was plain to see. Frank, bad breath, nasty manner, and all, took the boss's unspoken hint and faded quietly into the background.

"So this is the car you want?" Larry patted the hood of the red Jetta with affection. "Good car, this one. Get in, take a look around, see how it makes you feel." He opened the door and I climbed behind the wheel.

It felt good, like I had always been there. The upholstery was black, the same color as the Demon's, and I had a thrilling moment of déjà vu. It was a manual, too, which I like. Jake, who loves to drive almost as much as he loves to cook, says that driving a stick is like cooking with gas; you have control and the car will tell you what you're doing. He puts an automatic car in the same category as electric stoves—don't need it. At this point in my life, I wouldn't drive anything else.

"Feels good." I pressed down on on the clutch and shifted the gears, which were as smooth as silk.

"You like the color?"

"Love it. I never thought I'd like a red car, but I do," I said, suddenly remembering that red was Celia's color; it seemed fitting.

"How about a test drive?"

"I can do that?"

"Never buy a car without one."

The reality of my pocketbook brought me back to earth. "No, that's okay," I said as I climbed out of the car. "I really don't think this one is for me."

"How will you know if you don't try it? Hey, Frank, get me the keys to this thing, we're taking it out. Come on, Tamara, we're out of here." He handed me the keys Frank had promptly delivered.

As I sped on to the street, I felt the sheer pleasure of driving a car that yields to your every command. The Demon, with its stalls and quirks, had gotten me out of many a scrape, but there was always that dreadful moment when I had to claim it at parking lots, all those times I prayed it would start and spare me the humiliation of calling AAA for the fifth time that month. There would be none of that with this one. It glided onto the Garden State Parkway as if it were on skates. With a touch of the accelerator, I was in the left lane, leaving bigger, fancier cars in my wake. I whizzed past exits on the Parkway, barely slowing down for the toll gates. With style and panache, I finally rolled onto Route 280 and back into the streets of Newark, vaguely hoping that somebody I knew would spot me. When I drove into Rayson's Used Cars, I didn't want to return the keys.

"Great car," I mumbled as I handed them back to Larry.

"Your car. I can tell by the way you handle it."

"No, I'd better look around some more." I tried not to sound like a disappointed kid.

"How much you got to spend?"

"Not enough for this." I looked him in the eye for the first time since I'd gotten out of the car. "I can't afford this one, Larry. I didn't get much for my other car, which was totaled, and I can't afford to take anything else out of my savings."

"I didn't ask you all that, Tamara, I just asked you what you can afford to spend."

I told him and for the briefest moment, disappointment flashed in his eyes, but he recovered quickly. "I think we can work with that."

"Are you crazy?"

"Yeah, maybe, a little bit. Hey, it's a beautiful day, you're a beautiful lady, and we go *way* back."

He was right about that. We went further back even than the leavings of my fish sandwich on his lapel, and the irony of confronting my history with Celia struck me again.

He had been one of three popular seniors headed places most of the kids in my school would never see. They were all smart, athletic, fine, with the pick of any girl they wanted. The three of them ran the school, never held back by the boundaries that limited the rest of us. They called Larry "Chessman" because he loved the game and had won some hard-played matches with players from richer, better schools, bringing fame and pride to our city in the pages of the *Star-Ledger.*

He was the friendliest of the three, the only one who would look down from his perch to acknowledge me and Celia, although I suspected Celia had other dealings with one or all of them; there was something secretive about the way she acted when she was around them. But she never admitted to anything, and I never asked her. Even as kids, we respected each other's privacy. It wouldn't have surprised me, though. Like every other girl in the freshman class, we had crushes on all three. "Chessman" was my favorite, though. Maybe it was because he always remembered my name.

"High school was a long time ago," I said.

"Not as long as you might think." I wondered if something in his past was catching up with him, too.

"So whatever happened to your friends, those two guys you used to hang with? I'm sure you all went to college and did great, important things with your lives." I hadn't meant to sound cynical, and the look that shadowed his eyes made me wish I'd altered my tone.

He paused before he answered. "Clayton ended up a big-time judge. I used to see him and his wife a couple of times a year. He died a year ago last August. Drew and I are still very good friends. I see him at least once or twice a week. He went to pharmacy school and has ended up rich as all hell. Me, well you see where I am in life. All of us got married, had kids, me and Drew did anyway. Clayton and his wife weren't as blessed, and life goes on." His shrug of indifference didn't match his words. He wasn't good at hiding things, and I wasn't sure yet if that was good or bad.

"You have kids, then?" That was always a common point of entry to any conversation.

His face softened the way mine does when I mention Jamal. "A daughter. Nia. Almost ready to go to college and leave her old man forever." He chuckled self-consciously.

"An empty nest can be a good thing for a couple. Helps them get back in touch with each other." I'd heard that on some talk show and threw it out for lack of anything better to say.

"My wife and I are divorced. Well, you want the car, Ms. Hayle, or not?" He'd changed the subject abruptly but there was no nastiness in his tone, just an eagerness to get the deal done. It told me that the breakup of his marriage had been recent enough for him not to want to talk about it, but far enough in the past for some perspective.

We headed into his office to sign the papers, and I was able to purchase the car with a reasonable down payment and manageable monthly payments, thanks to his generosity.

"Tamara, I'd like to see you again, maybe meet for dinner or a drink, something that has nothing to do with cars," he said as we walked back to the lot.

His request for a date caught me short. I was tempted, but it didn't feel right.

"No, I don't think so," I said after a moment or two. My answer surprised him, and I could see that he was hurt. He wasn't a man who was used to being turned down by women; he hadn't been in high school and he obviously wasn't now. "Actually, I'm kind of involved with somebody," I added to soften my rejection.

That was a lie, of course. I haven't been "kind of involved with somebody" since I met a sexy "somebody" named Basil Dupre for a week of mayhem and lust in Atlantic City. I'm not sure when, if ever, that somebody will turn up in my life again. Our relationship has no rhyme or reason, and I've learned to accept it for what it is. There was nobody else except Jake, who shows up in my dreams, and I'm too much of a realist to live in my fantasies.

Yet on a deeper level, I *was* involved with somebody, and that somebody was me. I swore off men after I left Atlantic City. It was time for me to rediscover myself, cherish my own company, stop depending on somebody else to give meaning to my life. I had only a few more years at home with my son before he went to college, and I needed to focus on him, not romance. Besides that, it's never wise to mix business and pleasure. I've learned that in spades.

"He's a very lucky somebody."

"Thanks, Larry, for everything," I said without acknowledging his compliment. I climbed into my new red car, turned the key in the ignition, and headed to Morgan's Funeral Home, my grin so wide it hurt.

"D*on't let me be here all night* dealing with this shit, you hear me? Don't let me be here all night," said the woman to Brent Liston, who stood next to her. There was no mistaking the voice; it was the one I'd heard on the phone yesterday morning. The speaker had a sweet-looking face marred by a mouth that looked like it never smiled. She held her small, wiry body in a fighter's stance, which didn't surprise me, considering who had his arm swung over her shoulder like he owned her. So Cecil Jones had given me his father's telephone number; they must have been closer than I thought.

Once upon a time, Liston had been handsome in a brutal, machismo way. The twisted scar that ran down his left cheek and his squat, broken nose had changed all that, but he'd done enough time in prison gyms to still have the body of a contender. He was dressed all in black, save for a thick gold chain that crossed his tie. I noticed Cecil's diamond ring sparkling like a pimp's on his long, thick finger. Standing there together, he and his woman looked like they'd stepped out of somebody's nightmare.

When she spoke, the woman's voice carried to the back of the room, but she didn't seem to give a damn. She studied indifferently the rough, uncarpeted floor, red velvet pews, and stained-glass windows, which were designed to make the Rose Chapel, where the funeral would be held, look like a church even though there was nothing holy about the place. I was thankful she didn't spot me. Dressed as she was in her scruffy boots and cheap leather jacket, she looked like the kind of woman who would call me out by name before she knew it, and I sure didn't feel like getting into it with somebody like her today. Just walking into Morgan's Funeral Home had put me in a bad mood.

I'd buried half my family in this place, perched as it was between a gasoline station and convenience store on a busy street in the middle of town. Old Man Morgan, whose mournful expression could bring a clown to tears, spotted me and waved as he headed in my direction.

"Tamara Hayle! How are you, my dear. Has life been treating you well?" Morgan's voice always seemed to be on the verge of a sob, each sentence punctuated with a sorrowful nod. "And here I am again, putting away another one. Boy was just in here a month ago, burying his mama. Put her away a month ago, and here I am again."

My ears perked up. "So Cecil was the one who buried his mother?"

He looked at me as if just remembering I was there. "So you knew his mother?"

"We were friends."

"I don't remember seeing you at the service." He scowled with disapproval over his half-framed glasses.

"I was out of town," I stammered unconvincingly, then added truthfully, "I didn't know about it or I would have been here."

"Should have sent some flowers," he mumbled.

"Were there many people here?" I changed the subject.

"Not many. The boy. Two or three others. Not many at all. Violent deaths are always dreadful, but Celia Jones's was particularly bad. Poor woman was shot right through her—" He dropped his eyes as if embarrassed.

"Right through her what?"

"Well," he sighed and added after a beat, "near her belly. Not belly exactly, but her womb, the center of a woman's being. I figure that whoever did it was trying to make some kind of statement. I've never seen anything like it, to shoot a woman right through her privates."

"Do you mean that somebody put a gun—"

"I don't know how he did it, Miss Tamara." Morgan avoided my eyes as if the mere mention of the subject distressed him. "Maybe you should ask the police. They're the ones who did the autopsy. I just got the body, that's all I do—clean 'em, fix 'em, dress 'em up. I made her presentable so her son could say his last good-bye, but I sure could see where she'd been shot."

"Was she shot more than once?" I'd read as much, but I wanted Morgan's confirmation.

"I don't know, Miss Tamara. All I know is that the poor woman is dead. That's all I know and that's all I will say." He pursed his lips, indicating that he was uncomfortable with the subject. I wasn't about to let him go, but in deference to his discomfort went in a different direction.

"Do you see anyone here today who came to Celia's funeral?"

"How am I supposed to remember something like that?" He eyed me suspiciously trying to figure out what I was up to.

I broke out my professional voice. "As you know, Mr. Morgan, I make my living as a private investigator. I'm not just asking you these questions because I'm nosy, but because I've been hired to find out who killed Celia Jones, and in the process I may be able to find out who killed her son. I'd appreciate any help you could give me, anything at all."

"Who hired you?" Even after my little speech, Morgan was still skeptical.

"I'm not at liberty to say."

"Didn't the cops find out who did it?"

"No."

"Isn't that their job?"

"Often people are uncomfortable talking to the police, so they'll talk to me. Could you help me out? Please?" I pulled out the stops on the "please," my eyes begging him to recall the many funerals we'd shared.

"Well, I guess it won't do no harm for you to look and see who signed the register, but hardly nobody came. You can't take it with you though," he added as if I might try to steal it. "I'll leave it on my desk in my office, and you can look at it there. It's my property now since the boy is dead. I guess I can show it to you."

"That will be very helpful, Mr. Morgan. Thank you so much." I hugged him awkwardly, inhaling as I did so an odd mixture of breath mints and formaldehyde. He nodded toward the Rose Chapel. I settled into a dark corner of the last row, folded my hands piously in my lap, and watched things unfold.

They buried the boy in a cheap pine coffin, which I knew from personal experience was the bottom of Morgan's line. The coffin was open; he'd been stabbed through the heart, not the face, and Morgan had probably done a good job of fixing him up, as good a job as anybody can do on a dead body. I knew that from experience, too. Liston and his woman sat in the first row. His arm had slipped from her shoulder and was casually draped on the back of the seat as if they were waiting for cheeseburgers in a greasy luncheonette.

A child's piercing cries broke the silence in the room and drew everybody's attention to the back of the chapel. A young woman holding a wailing baby on her hip entered, accompanied by two young men who walked beside her like bodyguards. Cecil hadn't mentioned a child, but I assumed the baby was his. The woman, little more than a child herself, still carried the weight of her pregnancy, and her shiny gray suit and diaphanous blouse, both obviously bought when she was twenty pounds lighter, did little to hide it.

"Ooh this is bad! This is bad! This is so bad!" the girl kept repeating to nobody in particular.

"He dead and gone now, Cristal. There ain't nothing you can do now. Nothing you can do!" This bit of stage-whispered wisdom came from the shorter of the men. He wasn't as tall as Brent Liston, but looked a younger version of him—same powerful chest and shoulders, same bullying strut.

"Hey, Pik, there go his dad," said the other kid, who was thin with a delicate face that contrasted with the tough-guy clothes he wore.

He grinned inappropriately, and I noticed that his teeth were perfectly straight and lacked the gold and diamonds that usually distinguish the dental work of wannabe gangstas. I knew from the money I've spent on my son's mouth that teeth like that don't come cheap. I was struck, too, by the boy's use of the word "dad." It was what I called my father when I was a kid, and he spoke the word as if it carried good memories. It made me think that he wasn't as tough as he wanted folks to think. Pik, the Liston look-alike, had enough thug in him for both of them.

"That big dude is his old man, right, DeeEss?" said Pik, whose mouth was lit up like a chandelier.

"Yeah."

"Cecil used to say he looked like his mama, but I think he looks kind of like his daddy. He fine," said the girl, her voice deep and dreamy. Cristal had a small pointed face and long thick hair haphazardly caught up in a metallic scrunchie. She wasn't pretty in the conventional sense of the word, but carried herself with a hoochie-mama swagger that probably appealed to teenage boys. It was troubling that my son found her attractive, but then again, I've never been a teenage boy. Pik's name was stenciled onto his black leather jacket and I realized I'd seen it painted in red letters on the facades of half a dozen buildings in the city.

"Who that woman? His moms?" Pik asked.

"Somebody killed his moms," said DeeEss.

Brent Liston turned and stared at the three teenagers as they sat down in the row behind him. His gaze seemed to frighten the girl, and she pulled her baby close as if protecting him. Her fear was puzzling. Why did she think Brent Liston would harm his grandchild? I realized then that she might be sheltering the child from Liston's woman, whose hard, pebble-shaped eyes stared at her with hatred. My feelings toward the girl and her child softened. Maybe something of Celia Jones had survived after all.

The click of high heels on the uncarpeted floor signaled the arrival of a middle-aged woman in a chic black suit, but her step was hesitant and unsteady, as if she were ill or had had too much to drink. She sat down in the row behind the teenagers, but perched on the edge of her seat, as if ready to launch into flight. Her clothes whispered money: tailored silk suit, black Coach bag, Ferragamo pumps, diamond earrings. I felt that pang of jealousy I often feel when I spot some woman whose outfit cost more than my office rent. But I didn't envy this woman her looks. She'd been attractive once, but her pretty face was bloated and her eyes bloodshot and puffy. It was plain to see that liquor, rather than illness or years, had aged her.

DeeEss glanced back as she slid in behind him, and she gave him a tight smile, which brought a nod. They shared the same features—same slight, pointed nose, hazel eyes set in an oval face the color of coffee with too much cream, same thin elegant frame; booze hadn't altered the family resemblance. They were mother and son, yet they were an odd pair. Had she come to pay her last respects to her son's friend or had something else brought her?

A man with wire-rimmed glasses and a conservative haircut was sitting behind the well-dressed woman. I hadn't noticed him come in, so I assumed he'd come early. He was dressed in a tan sweater and jacket and dull gray trousers. I pegged him for a teacher or guidance counselor, somebody who knew the boy casually, wanted to pay his respects, and get the hell out as fast as he could. I hoped that he signed the guest book that Morgan had placed at the door. I made a mental note to look.

The last person to enter the place was Larry Walton. I pulled back into the shadows, dropping my head down like I was praying, but he was moving so fast, he wouldn't have noticed me anyway. He sat next to the woman in the suit and gave her a hug. She settled into his muscular body as if she belonged there. I shook my head in disgust.

Men. There was no telling about them. If you gave them half a chance, even the best of them could drive you as crazy as a flea. This man had asked *me* out not an hour before, and here he was cozying up to some woman in a funeral parlor. I was glad that good sense had prevailed and I'd turned him down, but I'd been flattered by the asking, and I'd been tempted.

When it came to men, I was about as lucky as a hot biscuit at a church supper. I felt an unwavering passion toward Basil Dupre, but he was never around long enough for me to establish anything but memories. I thought I might be in love with Jake Richards, but my sense of morality got in the way of my establishing anything with him other than friendship.

I've found out the hard way that all love and loose change will get you is a bus to Broad and Market. Personal ethics are all a woman has, and she would want to keep them as clean as her drawers. I respected Jake's marriage. As for Basil, I wasn't quite sure where to put him, so I didn't put him anywhere. The only man I was truly responsible to at this point in my life was my son, and until he left my home, I had to spend my time looking out for him. I'd be damned if I'd ever let him end up like Cecil Jones or the countless other young men who are gone before they're twenty.

My son's face came into my mind as the earnest young minister gave his eulogy, which I suspected he'd given at the funerals of other boys like this one. No one spoke after he sat down. Nobody stood up to speak of grief, love, or sorrow. There were no tears or fond memories.

I considered standing myself. Somebody needed to bring the memory of Celia into this place. I was almost on my feet, when Brent Liston broke the silence.

"I want you all to know, I swear before God, I will find out who done this thing to my son, and I will take care of him good. I swear before God, I will. I swear before God!" he said, then plunked his heavy body back down in his seat, his face distorted by rage.

"Shut up, Brent Liston. In Celia's name I curse you," the thin voice of the woman in the black suit rose to challenge his. Her words were slurred, but she stood straight and tall without wavering. "Celia Jones knew who and what you were, Brent, and I know what you did to her and her son, you'll be damned in hell for that. You'll be damned!"

Morgan, alarmed by the turn of events, rushed to the front of the room, begging for silence although the room was quiet again and filled with tension. He slammed down the lid of the coffin as if something evil was about to pop out, and motioned for the pallbearers to come take this child and his low-life mourners out of his place. Memories of another funeral I'd attended here years ago that turned into an ugly melee came back to me; I needed to leave that room as soon as I could. I quickly ducked into Morgan's office.

I searched his desk for the register, couldn't find it for a moment, then spotted it under a pile of undertakers' trade magazines. Honorable to the end, Morgan had probably tucked it away, hoping that I'd get discouraged and be on my way. I turned to the January entries and found Celia's name at the top of the page marked January 8. Only three people had bothered to sign the guest book. I wondered if others had shown up. Rebecca Donovan's name was written in elaborate script at the top of the page. Larry Walton's name followed hers. Was Rebecca Donovan the woman who sat next to him and the reason he attended both of these services? The last name on the page was Drew Sampson, who I assumed must be related to the Annette Sampson I'd left the message for on Friday. One Sampson in the book, the other at her funeral. How were they connected to Celia?

That question was on my mind as I shoved Morgan's book where he'd put it, so I didn't see Brent Liston enter the room or sense his presence until he came up behind me, grabbed my shoulder, and swung me around to face him. My first impulse was to slap him across his face, but he caught my hand midway and forced it to my side.

"You that bitch Rebecca Donovan, ain't you?" he said. His woman stood behind him, gloating the way somebody does when they know they have the better of you, and in that moment, I hated them both with everything in me. "Hey, Beanie, ain't she that Clayton Donovan bitch who was always in my face?"

Beanie. The name suited her well. She was tiny and hard, like a navy bean or a black-eyed pea. I glanced away from her, focusing on him.

"Take your filthy hands off me before I send you back to hell," I said, and he laughed in my face.

"No, baby, you got it wrong. This one ain't her. She ain't hincty enough to be Rebecca Donovan." Beanie stared at me, her head cocked to the side like a bird of prey waiting for its dinner.

"Who are you and what you doing here, at my boy's funeral?" Liston dropped his hands to his sides. His lips quivered, like a playground tough who has just had his ass kicked, which surprised me because I was no threat to him. But I did know one thing now: The woman with Larry Walton was not Rebecca Donovan.

"I knew Celia," I said, just as Larry Walton came into the room to stand beside me.

"You all right, Tamara?"

"I'm fine." He stared Liston down, letting him know in the way that men do that I had a male protector, for what that was worth. It was a language, however, that Liston understood. He looked Larry up and down, waited a moment or two to show he wasn't scared, then left with Beanie.

"Let me walk you to your car," Larry said.

"I'm fine!" I stepped away from him, my tone letting him know that although his presence might frighten Liston, it didn't impress me. One way or the other I would have handled it myself.

"You're not as tough as you think. They might come back. Let me walk you to your car."

"That's really not necessary. I'm fine," I said, but he followed me anyway. We didn't say much as we walked toward the car. I didn't look at him as I unlocked the door and climbed in.

"I need to talk to you," he said.

I started my car. "About what?"

"About Celia and her boy. What are you doing now?"

"Going to pick up my son."

"How about later? Can I call you?"

I thought about it for a minute, wondering what he could tell me and if it would be worth my time. "Okay," I finally said.

I was halfway down the street before I realized I hadn't given him my telephone number. Then I remembered that my number, address, and every other bit of personal information that he needed to know about me was laid out on the top of his desk in triplicate.

CHAPTER SIX

"Ever heard of a guy named Larry Walton?" I asked my friend Jake Richards. We were sitting at his kitchen table drinking red wine. After my run-in with Brent Liston, I needed something stronger, but manners and the fear of looking like a lush prevented me from asking. Jake dropped his eyes the way he does when he thinks, and I took the opportunity to gaze at his face. He got better with age. The gray in his hair and beard gave him a distinguished, wise demeanor, yet still managed to play up the kindness in his eyes. He had the kind of face I could never get tired of looking at.

"No, I can't say that I have."

"What about Brent Liston?"

"Jesus, Tam, I hope you're not having dealings with him?" He sipped his wine and scowled, which made me smile.

"Well . . ."

He laughed despite himself. "Try to stay out of trouble, Tamara."

"I'm already in it."

"What am I going to do with you?" I was tempted to tell him, but swallowed some wine instead.

"So what do you know about him?"

"He is bad news, as simple as that. One of my guys defended him on an assault charge, and he got pissed at the way the judge ruled and threatened to beat the dude up. Like I said, bad news. He hasn't threatened you, has he?" His forehead wrinkled with concern, which reminded me of Jamal and his need to protect me.

"No, not really. What about Rebecca Donovan? Ever heard of her?"

"Is she related to Clayton Donovan?"

"I don't know."

"What does she look like?"

"I haven't seen her yet, but I think she's what some people might call 'hincty.' "

Jake laughed. " 'Hincty'? I haven't heard that one in a while, but I guess that's probably what some folks would call the honorable judge's wife. I don't know if that's what I'd call her, but Rebecca is the quintessential judge's wife in the 'here come da judge' tradition. She was, anyway. How is she involved in this?"

"I don't know yet. So they're divorced?"

"No, she's widowed. He died last August."

"Was he murdered?" The thought that Brent Liston could somehow be tied to the judge's demise crossed my mind.

"Judge Donovan? No. Died in bed, in a hospital. Walking pneumonia." Jake shuddered slightly, like a man reminded of his own mortality. "I argued a case before him on a Monday and was at his funeral a week later. Shook everybody up. Everybody."

"You liked him then."

Jake shrugged noncommittally. "As much as you can like somebody who was crazy as all hell and just this side of shady. The judge pushed the limits. Took chances. Rode the wild side, as they say. Sky diving, Harley, the whole bit. But he was always fair to me. A lot of the prosecutors used to say he ruled for the bad guys because he identified with them, but when he threw the book at somebody he threw it hard."

"And Rebecca was the lady who cleaned up his messes?"

Jake thought for a moment. "There really wasn't all that much to clean up. If the judge was anything, he was discreet. There was a lot of whispering about his carrying-on, but very little proof. Word was, he was a lady's man in spades, and he liked his women cut from the same cloth as him—a little crazy, a little shady with a touch of wildness. There was a young assistant DA who was carrying on with him for a while. But it didn't last long. He's the kind of man who plays at night, but always goes home to mama in the morning; he would never leave his wife. Rebecca Donovan was definitely the angel to his devil. So why are you so interested in the late Judge Donovan?"

"No reason."

"This isn't connected to Brent Liston, is it? He was one of those dudes who got the book tossed upside his head."

"What did he do to make the judge mad?"

"I don't know, but it must have been something bad. The brother had just done time for murdering a family member, and the judge sent him back on an assault charge for another few years. He just got out of prison a couple of months ago."

I filed that away for later reference.

"So you're not going to tell me why you're interested in Donovan?"

"I think I might have known him in high school," I said, connecting the Clayton Donovan that Jake just mentioned with the Clayton that Larry Walton said had been his friend. "He ran with Larry Walton, part of a trio of guys who were the hottest things around. At least in high school."

"So the name of Larry Walton comes back again. I'm not surprised Donovan was popular in high school. Some folks are born charismatic, and he was one of them."

"Have you ever heard of Annette Sampson? How about Aaron Dawson?"

Jake laughed. "Wow, baby! What are we playing here, twenty questions? Come on, Tam, I don't know everybody in Newark. Most folks don't come anywhere near my radar. Is Annette Sampson married to Drew Sampson?"

"Yeah, I think she is," I said, remembering his name in Morgan's guest book.

"Now *that* name, Drew Sampson, is familiar. So you're working on a new case?" He refilled my glass and then his own. "And this case is paying well," he added. Jake worries about my finances almost as much as I do.

"The client is deceased." I avoided his eyes.

"Deceased! I assume said client paid you before he died."

"More or less."

"More or less? Tamara, you've got to do better than that."

"I know," I said, like a recalcitrant child.

"Listen, I've recommended you to a guy I know, a very rich guy I might add, who is looking for somebody good to do some work for him. You ever heard of Francis B. Cosey?"

"Isn't he that big-time developer from Short Hills?"

"Yeah. He said you did some work for a friend of his, Sam Henderson, on a divorce case he was handling, and Henderson is still singing your praises. I told him I was certain you'd take the job. Hope you don't mind. Call him as soon as you can, and it's yours."

"So Cosey's getting a divorce?"

"No, corporate stuff, boring but it pays, and you won't have any losers like Brent Liston drifting into your life. But the case will take some time, and he'll need you a week from next Monday or the deal is no good. Are you going to be finished with this craziness by then?"

"Craziness?"

"If it involves Liston that's what it is. I assume you'll be ready by then, right?"

Jake is tender-hearted, but he's practical, and the look he gave me told me I would *want* to be finished with whatever I was doing in a week and a half. I knew he was right. He knew and I knew I had to start packing away some serious money for college. Soon I would have to let Celia and her wayward son drop back into my past.

"Yeah, I'll be finished one way or the other."

"You've got to be. Since you're obviously not doing whatever you're doing for the money, why is it so important?"

"Remember Celia Jones?"

He looked puzzled for a moment, then his eyes softened the way everyone's eventually did when her name came up. "From high school, yeah. She was younger than me, about your age, right? I remembered the name because I had an aunt named Celia, and I loved Celia Cruz. I read in the paper that she was killed."

"Murdered and so was her son, Cecil. He came to see me a couple of days before he died with a retainer to find his mother's killer."

"So I take it her son is your deceased client. I remember now. The kid was killed last week. He was around the same age as Jamal so it made an impression. Another bad day for our side." He shook his head, as he often did when remarking on "bad days" for his beloved city. "Listen, a cop I know is working on the kid's murder. Red. You might remember him as Griffin, from when Hakim was killed."

I did recall him and along with that memory came the sorrow that always comes when I remember the murder of Hakim, Jamal's best friend and half brother. Jake still bore a physical scar; Jamal and I carried ours in our hearts. Griffin remembered my brother Johnny and had gone out of his way to be helpful and kind to me and my son on that terrible day. As far as I was concerned, Griffin had a special pew in heaven. Jake wrote down Griffin's telephone number on the back of an envelope and gave it to me.

"He may be able to give you a sense of where the case for the son is going. Tell him I told you to call him, but he probably remembers you anyway. Hey, Tam, be careful!"

His words of caution made me grin. "Hey, Jake, I'm always careful!"

That made *him* grin, which I love to see because it lights up his whole face and when you see it, you know everything is going to be okay. And if it's not, he'll make it so. We sat there grinning at each other for a minute enjoying each other's company. Until the front doorbell rang and Jake answered it. Then the grin dropped off my face. My intuition told me who it was. I gulped down what remained of my wine; I'd need the fortification.

Ramona Covington swished into Jake's kitchen as if she belonged there. Although I didn't like to admit it, she was an undeniably attractive woman. Her short hair framed her pretty, square-jawed face in a style that said whoever wielded those scissors knew what he was doing. Her light-brown eyes were made up so flawlessly they looked natural, and her cherry red lips told me lipstick had just been applied. She was dressed casually, and her red cashmere sweat suit, if you could call it that, showed off the finer points of her well-toned body in sexy detail. Obviously surprised at my presence, she tossed me a grimace that only a fool could mistake for a smile and turned to Jake.

"So where have *you* been? I missed talking to you last night," she didn't so much say as purr as she settled into the chair next to him, crossing her legs seductively. I noticed with annoyance that there was nary a spot on her blindingly white sneakers.

Jake looked mildly embarrassed. I wasn't sure if it was because of what she said or my hearing it. "At a game."

"Game?" she asked as if she'd never heard the word before.

"Basketball. I took Jamal, Tamara's son, to see the Nets. Big fun. Nets won."

Has he rhymed the words intentionally or did her presence have that effect on him?

"Oh, that's right, you mentioned it. So you're Jamal's mom." She turned to me with a phony smile.

And you're the bitch from hell, I thought.

"Yes, we've met before," I mumbled, pulling my lips into what probably resembled a sneer.

"Oh, that's right! I remember now," she said, her condescending smile assuring me how easily forgettable I was. "How nice to see you again."

There was no need to dignify *that* remark with a response so we simply gazed at each other in awkward silence until Ramona turned her attention back to Jake, essentially sweeping me from the room with a toss of her head. There seemed to be no graceful way for me to enter their conversation, so I watched them without saying anything, desperately trying to figure out what this woman really meant to my friend.

Ramona Covington had popped into Jake's life a couple of years ago. She was a hotshot young prosecutor who left Trenton for Newark because she'd heard that Newark was where the action was. They were both lawyers, so they had that in common, and Jake liked smarts and spunk in women, so I knew he admired her. He'd never actually said there was anything romantic between them, but I could feel the chemistry, and where there's smoke, fire usually smolders. There was smoke between me and Jake, too, but we've always smothered any flames. I suspected that he and Ramona were sleeping together, but I wasn't sure. I did know, however, that Jake Richards was and had always been a gentleman. There wasn't a cruel or arrogant bone in his body, and I knew he would be too polite to tell her to get lost. But I sensed he probably wouldn't want to. I was also sure that she was a woman who wouldn't take "no" lightly. She was the kind of person who always got what she wanted, be it a job, a prime piece of real estate, or somebody else's husband. Ramona Covington had the instincts of a predator, and Jake Richards was fair game for a woman who put relationships with men in the same category as hunting and fishing.

Jake loved his wife, Phyllis, and I'd seen him through many of her "spells" as he called them. There was always sorrow in his eyes when she was around, an edginess that shadowed whatever he did. He seemed relaxed this evening, so I knew Phyllis was in the "rest home" where she goes when she gets overwhelmed by things that most of us handle easily. Phyllis had always been a fragile woman who brought out the protector in her husband. I admired him for both his love for her and his loyalty.

Even if I could, I'd never try to step into her shoes. Although there have been times when Jake and I have nearly crossed the line that separates friendship from something else, one of us has always pulled back. We both know that if we took that step, it would be impossible to come back to what we have, and we both value our friendship. Neither of us wants to lose the relationship that nurtures both of us as well as Jamal and Jake's daughter. Jake and I are truly comfortable with each other, and that is no small thing to be with a man.

But much to my annoyance, I had to admit that I was jealous of Ramona and her relationship with Jake. She had a clear advantage over me because she didn't give a damn about Phyllis and had no respect for Jake's marriage. She sensed his loneliness and swooped around him like a buzzard on the trail of a wounded animal. Ramona Covington was the kind of woman who couldn't be trusted with another woman's man. I knew that about her, and she knew I did. And she didn't like it. But most men do not want to hear your opinion about where they put their dicks. In short, whatever relationship Jake had with the woman was none of my business, and he would probably tell me so if I said anything. Wiser to keep my mouth shut and gather the chips when they fell.

"Ma, when did you get here?" Jamal busted into the room and came to my rescue.

"I've been here a while."

"Hey, Ms. Covington, how are you doing?" He graced Ramona with one of his winning smiles.

So just how many times has he seen her here? I wondered.

"Hi, Jamal. I heard the game was great," Ramona said with a 100-kilowatt grin. Add a few years and *Jamal* would be in her cross-hairs.

"Yeah. They're probably going to make the finals."

For one terrible moment, I thought he might ask her to accompany him and Jake to the next game. "Ready to go, Mom?"

"Whenever you are, son."

"Oh, yeah, I forgot to tell you. I was supposed to go by Charlie's tonight to work on that science project. Can you drop me off on the way home?"

"Science project? When's it due?" Concern was in Jake's voice.

"Monday."

"Jamal!" Jake and I said in unison.

"Yeah, I'm going to spend the night. Got my toothbrush!" He pulled out one of the spare toothbrushes Jake kept in the house and waved it in front of us, trying to put us at ease.

Jake scowled. "Last minute don't get it, brother-man! You should have done that project instead of going to the game."

"We're going to work all night." Jamal pleaded for understanding.

Jake looked doubtful.

"Really!" Jamal added.

Jake glanced at me and rolled his eyes, which made me smile.

"Let's go. The sooner you get there the sooner you can get started," I said.

"Catch you later," Jamal said to Jake, giving him the half-hug that men give one another.

"You, too, man." Jake grinned to let him know that all was forgiven. "Check with you later on tonight, Tam?"

I didn't answer for a moment. I could hear the affection and concern he had for me, and I knew that he probably had something he had to talk to me about; maybe Phyllis, maybe his daughter, maybe even the feelings he had—or didn't have—for Ramona Covington. But I was mad that she was there, and I didn't want him to know it.

"Actually I have plans for tonight," I said breezily, avoiding his eyes as Jamal and I left.

I'm not sure where that lie came from, probably the same place as the one I'd told Larry Walton. Fortunately for me, Jamal was so overwhelmed by the sight of our new car, he forgot to ask me what those plans were.

"Wow!" he said when I pointed out the new Jetta, dashing toward it like a kid heading for the tree on Christmas morning. "And it's red, too! Ma, this is dope! This is dope!" I buzzed open the door for him and he jumped in, grinning so wide it made me chuckle. "Ma, wow. You really did it this time. You can even open it by remote. You really did it! I can't wait to drive this thing."

"You'll wait until you get your license."

"Soon, Ma, soon," he said, which made me sigh. One more thing to worry about: Jamal on the road. He patted the dashboard as if it were alive. "This is way better than the Demon."

"That wouldn't take much," I said, and we both laughed at the fond memory of our trusted old car.

"Open it up!"

"I'm not going to 'open it up' in the city. A ticket would be all I need."

"Let's go on the Parkway. If we have enough time. What time is your date?"

I didn't answer him. One bold-faced lie an hour was enough. I headed to the Parkway, shifting into fourth, then fifth, glancing in my rearview mirror to make sure I was clear of cops. It was fun chasing down the highway cheered on by my son as our car rang with his laughter. But my feelings were bittersweet because I knew how short the time left between us would be. After "opening it up" to Jamal's satisfaction, I dropped him off at his friend's house with a peck on his cheek and a quick scolding about the dangers of procrastination. I drove into my driveway, then sat there for a while, thinking about Jamal and how much I would miss him, about Jake and how I'd lied to him, and then, for some reason, about Larry Walton. I was smiling, though, as I got out of my car and headed into my house. I had a new car, a great kid, and, courtesy of a good friend, a job that would pay me good money in a week and a half. I had seen better days in my life, but I sure had seen worse.

My self-satisfied grin was still on my face as I turned the lock and came into my kitchen. Then I stopped short; something was wrong. Someone had been in my house. Small things were out of place: The chair that leans against the wall had been turned to the right. The blue glass jars that hold my sugar and flour were pushed away from the wall. The tablecloth was askew, the window cracked, the door-mat pushed to the left.

My heart pounded. I held my breath.

Was he still here?

"I'm warning you, I've got a gun and I'm licensed to use it!" I made my voice sound tough, threatening, but I had no gun. It was locked in a safe in my bedroom. I was scared, and the tremble in my voice gave me away because I wanted to turn tail and run.

But was I imagining things?

Could Jamal have left the chair pushed out, the tablecloth crooked, the doormat out of place. I had been in a rush to buy the car this morning, maybe I simply hadn't noticed.

Trust your instincts.

That had been drilled into me so often when I'd been a cop, I said it in my sleep.

Always trust your gut.

My place had been violated. I was sure of it now, but by whom? And what was he looking for? Had he known I wouldn't be home? Or had he been looking for me? Was he still here?

I stepped farther into the kitchen, my ears alert for any sound, my eyes searching for any sudden movement. I grabbed a butcher knife out of the knife holder next to the blue glass containers, stepped carefully, the knife tight in my hand, ready to use it if I needed to.

Silence.

Slowly, I climbed the stairs, listening for sounds, glancing behind me, all my senses sharpened. The smell was different. It was an odor from my past, heavy like perfume, but I wasn't sure where and when I had smelled it before. I stood there trying to identify it, but I couldn't remember. I entered my bedroom, scared as hell, and went to the locked chest that held my gun. My fingers shook as I turned the combination, opened the chest, picked up the gun, and clicked off the safety. Then I searched my house—Jamal's room, closets, under the beds, basement—my .38 in one hand, kitchen knife in the other.

I found nothing and after a while I felt foolish for having been so afraid. I placed the knife back in the holder, locked the gun back up, then collapsed on the couch, my body tense. I thought of calling Jake, then dismissed the thought. The telephone rang, the jarring sound of it startling me. It rang four times before I answered it.

"Tamara?"

"Who is this?"

"Larry Walton. I said I'd call you later, remember?"

"Yeah."

"I was wondering if you're free tomorrow. For brunch."

"Yeah."

"How about Jay's in Newark, is that okay? Let's say around one?"

"Yeah," I said, and hung up the phone, my fingers as tight around it as they'd been around the gun.

I'm not sure what made me pick up the pencil lying next to the phone and write the letters I'd seen in Celia's book on a scrap of paper. I don't know why the letters came out in the girlish script that had been in her book, as if her hand were guiding mine.

A. *Was it for Annette or Aaron?*

B. *Brent? Beanie? Both?*

C. D. *Clayton Donovan?*

Or was C for Chessman?

asked *Larry Walton about* Celia Jones the moment we sat down to brunch.

"Do you mind if we order first?" he asked with the charming grin that marked everything he said. He was a good-looking man, that was for sure, and the teenage waitress acknowledged it with a nauseatingly sweet smile as she set our table. He ordered brunch like he was serious about food, which is always a good sign in a man. Jay's was jammed, like it is every Sunday morning. I usually throw caution to the wind when I come here, wolfing down calories and carbs like they won't show up on my hips, but even the fried fish and biscuits didn't tempt me this morning.

As Larry Walton sipped his orange juice, I gulped down the first of three cups of coffee lined up in a row in front of me. It was tacky as hell to order three cups at once, but I needed the jolt and didn't feel like waiting for refills. Last night had been another rough one. I spent the first half of the night tossing, turning, and waiting for somebody to try to break into my place again, and the second half trying to figure out what Larry was going to say to me this morning.

"You sure you don't want anything else?" he asked as the waitress set down his order of eggs, biscuits, fried porgies, and grits. The smell of fried fish has always had the power to break me, but professional integrity beat out greediness this morning. It was better not to let him treat me to brunch until I knew what role he played in Celia's drama, and I didn't want to pay for it myself; brunch at Jay's was not in my budget.

"No, I'm fine," I said.

He grinned, dimple showing. "That's what you told me yesterday. When aren't you 'fine,' Tamara Hayle? Is there ever a time when you aren't self-sufficient and self-reliant?"

"I'm fine then, and I'm fine now." I hadn't meant to sound so snappish, but it came out that way, and I didn't bother to apologize. Larry shrugged as if it didn't matter and bit into a biscuit. Neither of us spoke until he'd finished eating, and I asked the question that had been bothering me since yesterday afternoon.

"So why were you at both of their funerals?"

He took a sip of coffee, placed the cup carefully down on the table, and looked me in the eye.

"You mean Celia and her son?"

"Why else are we here?"

"Because I knew Celia."

"In the biblical sense?" I asked, hurled into nastiness by three cups of coffee on an empty stomach. "So just how close were you?"

"Close enough so I cared about her and Cecil. Close enough so that if I had ten minutes alone with the son of a bitch who killed her, they'd put me in jail for life," he said in a way that told me more than he knew. "I was at loose ends for a while. Marva, my wife, and I were still together, but I was very lonely, and being lonely in a bad marriage is the worst kind of loneliness. I was looking for someone to help me through a bad time. I needed some fun, and my relationship with Celia supplied both."

"So basically, you just fucked her," I said, using the "F" word to both shock and bluntly define what I suspected was at the core of their relationship. It had the desired effect: He blushed and dropped his gaze for a moment before returning his eyes to mine.

"I suppose that some people might put it like that, but Celia was very vulnerable and kinder than anybody I've met in a very long time," he said, implying with a slightly raised eyebrow that she had it on me in the kindness department. "Celia Jones was a decent woman who never got a break, and during the time I was with her, I treated her like a queen because beneath all that tough bravado, that's what she was.

"I wasn't in love with Celia, and she certainly wasn't in love with me, she had too many other men in her life for that, and she made no secret of it, but I respected and liked her, and I hope she felt the same about me. Fucking her, as you put it, was a very small part of our relationship."

It was my turn to blush. For a minute, I thought he was going to stand up and stomp out of the place. Instead, he politely asked if I'd like some more coffee, and ordered another cup for himself, keeping me on tenterhooks as he added cream and sugar and leisurely stirred it.

"So do you still play chess?" I asked, sick of the strained silence and trying for neutral ground.

He was surprised by the question. "Yes, once a chess player always a chess player. It's a game that influences your life."

I couldn't think of a follow-up to that so I asked the obvious. "Why did you invite me to brunch?"

"When I saw you yesterday, I remembered you'd been Celia's friend in high school. I figured you'd cut her out of your life like everybody else, so I didn't bring her name up, but when you came to her son's funeral I knew that at least you'd cared enough about the two of them to show up. I asked you out because I wanted to find out if you had any idea who could have killed her or her son. Will you tell me what you know?"

It's always tough to tell if somebody is leveling with you or simply tossing out a bunch of crap to see how much you know about a given situation. That was one thing I learned in my short stint as a cop: Never immediately believe what somebody says, search for the forgotten detail that will point to the truth, don't take anyone at his word. My bullshit meter is usually pretty accurate, but the needle was jumping all over the place this morning. The only person who could verify what Larry'd told me about him and Celia was dead. I didn't answer his question, but came from another direction.

"So was Celia the reason you and your wife broke up?"

"No. Me and Marva parted ways a long time before I started going out with Celia."

"When did you start your relationship with her?"

"About three years before she died."

"Could your wife have had it in for Celia?"

It was the first time he'd laughed since we sat down, yet his eyes didn't reflect his amusement. "Marva? No. She left me for a preacher man a year before Celia was killed. Took my daughter, Jamillah, and moved with him to Nashville. She married him the day our divorce was final. She was pregnant with his baby last time I saw her. Marva has cut out a new life for herself, and I'm happy for her."

"Did *you* blame Celia for breaking up your marriage?"

"Celia didn't break up my marriage. My wife was a good woman and she deserved better from me than she got. Next time I hold a piece of gold, I'll know how to polish it."

"You mentioned other men in Celia's life. Was one of them Drew Sampson?" I asked, aiming wildly, hoping to hit something. I realized now that the Drew he'd mentioned as one of his best friends in high school must be the same Drew Sampson who had signed Morgan's guest book and was connected to Annette Sampson. The look in his eyes told me I'd hit it.

"Drew Sampson? Why are you bringing him into this?" His brow wrinkled into a frown.

"No reason. I just saw his name in Celia's diary," I said, stretching the truth.

He looked puzzled, "So you *are* investigating Celia's murder then."

I gave him the truth. Or part of it anyway. "She was a friend of mine. We shared some history. I thought I'd ask around a little bit."

"I've heard you're a good detective."

"I have my days."

"Will you keep me abreast of what you find out? I don't mind paying you."

"I've already been paid, thank you."

He looked confused, then went back to Drew Sampson. "So Celia kept a diary. Wow! I'm surprised Drew's name is in it. Drew is probably one of the best friends I have, and to tell the truth, I don't think he's looked at another woman since he married Annette. He spends too much time counting his money from those drugstores to—"

"Drew Sampson is Sampson Drugs?" I asked with new respect, as I connected his name to the chain of small independent drugstores that had sprouted up in neighborhoods where the big guys wouldn't go.

"The same, but not for long. He just sold it, and he got a very big check from a very big corporation. He told me a couple of days ago that he's getting the hell out of Newark. Too many bad memories here."

"Bad memories? Like what?"

He shrugged, suddenly uncomfortable. "A lot of things have changed in Newark in the past few years." The tone in his voice reminded me of Jake's when he talked about the way the city was growing, and that caught me by surprise.

"Not fast enough for some," I said.

"Faster than they thought it would after the riots."

"The riots were a long time ago."

"Not as long ago as you think," Larry said with a chuckle, and I left my pursuit of the truth long enough to share the affection and concern I have for our city. We spoke of the city's rebirth and our excitement about what might yet happen. We laughed about local characters we both remembered who had made the city what it was. After about ten minutes of shared remembrances, I brought the conversation back to where I wanted it.

"So Drew was sick of Newark and the life he had here."

"Drew took a lot from Newark, but he gave a lot back, too. He and Annette contributed to every charity there was, and he served on half a dozen boards. He wrote more checks for benefits than most folks pay in rent."

"Where does he want to go?"

"I'm not sure. Fiji, maybe. New Zealand, places he's only read about. His grandmother was Cuban, and he talks about her a lot. He says he'd like to see Cuba before he dies."

"He's retiring, then."

"To tell the truth, Drew was always more interested in making money than making people healthy, and now that he's made a lot of it, he just wants to relax. He's a pharmacist with a broad knowledge of drugs. I call him whenever I need anything. But he's also a very astute businessman."

"Do you know why he showed up at Celia's funeral? His name was on the guest list."

He studied me for a moment as if deciding whether to level with me, then said, "He was looking for his wife. He knew that Annette would probably see the register, and he wanted her to know that he was there. At least Marva left me for another man. Drew wasn't the one involved with Celia, it was Annette. She left him for Celia Jones. It shocked the hell out of me, too," he said, acknowledging the expression on my face. "I had no idea Celia swung both ways, as they say, but she was a free spirit, and she must have had that effect on Annette as well."

"It must have shocked the hell out of Drew Sampson, too."

"Shock was the least of it. Annette took their son, Drew Junior, and moved back to her father's old place with Celia and her boy. Annette has a bit of the social worker in her, and according to Celia, she was trying to help her get her life together, which Celia both appreciated and resented."

"So Celia told you about their relationship?"

"Celia and I were friends. I looked out for her son as much as I could, until Annette came into the picture. I loaned her money when she needed it. But Annette was extremely possessive, which really pissed off Celia. Annoyed the hell out of me, too."

"She and Celia were together when Celia was murdered?"

"I'm not sure."

"Annette didn't go to her funeral, at least she didn't sign the guest book."

"I usually don't bother signing those things either, do you?"

"But you signed the one at Celia's funeral."

"I signed it for the boy, so he'd have a record of who cared enough about his mother to pay their last respects. I don't know why Annette did or didn't sign. Yesterday was the first time I'd seen her in months."

"So that was Annette Sampson you were sitting next to? I thought it might be Rebecca Donovan. Brent Liston mistook me for her."

"Liston mistook you for Rebecca? No way!" He laughed at that, too, and his expression told me that according to whatever criteria he was using, I came out the better.

"So the kid at the funeral, the one sitting in front of you and Annette, was her son, right?" I asked, although I'd already guessed it.

"DeeEss, he calls himself these days. He was a nice middle-class boy for a while, Jack and Jill, the whole bit, but he's definitely taken a turn in another direction. Cecil's influence, I'm sad to say. The kid's world blew apart when Annette fell in love with Celia. If you ask me, what she did was pretty damned selfish."

"But you never know what is *really* going on in a marriage," I said, speaking as much from experience as anything else. When I'd been married to DeWayne Curtis, I'd done so much smiling through tears my jaws got cramped.

He nodded, agreeing with me. "Yeah, but I would have fought her for the kid. Annette and Drew had what they call a traditional marriage. Drew made the money, ran the business, and she took care of the house, raised the kid, so it was natural the boy would go with her when she left. He and his father weren't all that close, although Drew loves that boy with all his heart. It was strange, though, what happened. Annette always seemed pretty happy to me," he said, then added a moment later in retrospect, "according to Drew anyway. He blamed Celia for corrupting her, as he put it."

"So he blamed Celia for losing his wife and son?"

"That's what he's always said. I've tried to explain to him that he couldn't blame Celia for something like that, but he insisted that she's to blame."

When I heard that, Drew Sampson's name went in red to the top of my most-likely-suspects list.

"It seems to me that Sampson's sense of what was going on in his wife's head was about as clear as a smoky day in hell. Did Annette have a job? She must have done something when she wasn't ironing, cooking, and cleaning his house."

Larry looked embarrassed, and I was amused again about how little the average man knows about the inner life of the average woman. Annette as "person" outside of "wife and mother" had completely escaped him. It took him a moment to come up with something.

"Come to think about it, Annette was an aspiring artist. She was very involved with the Newark Museum for a while, and one of her paintings was in a group show at a gallery for emerging artists. That was a couple of years ago, though. Look, Tamara, maybe you'd better talk to Drew and Annette about their business. If they'll talk to you."

"I suspect Drew's number is unlisted. Do you have a number for him?"

He looked so uncomfortable, I didn't pursue it, but asked instead, "So did *you* introduce Annette to Celia?"

"Me? No. I was as surprised as Drew when she upped and left with Celia. Celia had mentioned she was involved in a new relationship that was going to be good for her, but she didn't say who it was with. She never mentioned names."

"And you were still seeing her at that point?"

He hesitated before he answered; his expression revealed that he wasn't sure if this was any of my business. I stared him down, as if I had a perfect right to know.

"Tamara, I think you should understand that my relationship with Celia took place a number of years before she was murdered. I looked out for her kid as much as I could, talked to her when she needed somebody to talk to, but I realized early on that I needed more from a woman than Celia was willing to give." He smiled sadly and shook his head. "I suspect Celia had quite a few relationships between the time that we were intimate and when she got involved with Annette Sampson."

I made a point of picking up my cup and drinking the last bit of coffee as I tried to decide the best way to phrase my last question, the one I was sure would end our conversation, probably on a bad note

"So, uh, did the cops talk to you when Celia was murdered?" I looked him in the eye, trying to spot any truth he was hiding.

He looked genuinely puzzled. "Me? No. Like I said, my thing with Celia happened three years ago. Are you asking me if I killed Celia?"

"Well, uh, I'm trying to figure out how good a job the cops did, who they talked to, what leads . . ." I sputtered on, a phony smile fixed on my lips. Larry rescued me from myself.

"Well, Tamara, here's the answer to the question you're not comfortable asking. I was visiting my daughter in North Carolina the day of Celia's death. I read about it in the paper the next day like everybody else. Here's Marva's number so you can check out my alibi." He jotted down his wife's telephone number on a napkin and pushed it across the table toward me. "As for Cecil, I was down in DC doing a deal with a guy who sold me a fleet of cars, one of which I sold you. I don't have his number, but it's in my office. I'll leave it on your machine so you'll have that, too. The police didn't ask about my whereabouts when Celia was killed because I'm not a suspect, and I never have been. I'm amazed that you could possibly think that I could have something to do with that poor woman's death."

And with that, he paid the bill and left.

The memory of the kid hit me the moment I walked into my office the next morning. It had been only a week since he'd been sitting here with his tough little self, Celia's ghost trailing right behind him. I snapped on my computer, determined to put them out of my mind and do something constructive. By the time the screen lit up, I couldn't think of squat to write, so I went through my usual procrastination—made some tea, watered the orphan aloe, gazed out my dirty window.

I thought about Larry Walton and checked for a message with the telephone number of the car dealer in DC, but he hadn't bothered to leave it. Chances were his alibi would have checked out anyway or he wouldn't have mentioned it. I called Cosey, Jake's contact about the job, and told him I was interested. He hired me on the spot, explaining that I'd have to start the following Monday, which was fine with me. I remembered that Jake had scribbled the number of the detective on an envelope and searched through my Kenya bag for it, then cursed out loud when I realized I'd left it on my kitchen table. I considered calling him to get it, then admitted to myself that it would simply be a ruse to talk to him and waste more time.

When the phone rang, I answered it on the first ring.

"Ms. Tamara Hayle? Rebecca Donovan here, returning your call. My answering service said you called on Friday, and I wanted to get back to you." She sounded efficient, like a woman who didn't like to waste your time and expected the same courtesy from you. I was tempted to ask her about her hoity-toity answering service but changed my mind. It was best to get right to the point.

"Oh, yes. Ms. Donovan. Thank you so much for calling me back." I tucked the phone between my shoulder and chin and grabbed my notebook and pen. "I was calling about Celia Jones."

"Celia Jones?" She paused and sounded puzzled, as if trying to place the name, then added, "Celia Jones is dead. I believe she died in January. There's absolutely nothing I can tell you."

The note of dismissal in her voice told me she was preparing to hang up so I quickly added, "Yes, I'm aware of her death, but I've been hired to look into her murder."

She gave a slight, well-mannered gasp. "Someone actually hired you to look into that woman's death? I can't imagine who would do that. I assumed that the police were investigating it. Isn't the trail cold by now?"

"It's hot again. The murder of her son warmed it up." I sounded more sure than I was. I couldn't gauge the effect of my bravado, but it brought a momentary pause, after which she said, "Well, I'll certainly help you in any way that I can."

"Thank you for your cooperation. So how did you and Celia meet?"

"I was a volunteer at a women's shelter. Celia was a person trapped in a rat's hole of a life, and my heart went out to her. As a child, I was taught to always help people in need, that it was the right thing to do, so I offered her as much aid as I could. I'm afraid, though, she needed far more than I was able to give. I was, however, able to help her get away from the father of her son."

"You're referring to Brent Liston?"

"Yes."

"How did you help her get away from him?"

There was silence, then a sigh. "Through my husband, Clayton. I'm the widow of the Honorable Clayton Donovan. He passed away last August. Very suddenly."

"Oh yes, I was sorry to hear that."

Another sigh. "There's not much else I can tell you." She cleared her throat. "If my husband were still alive, he might be able to be of help but—"

"Do you know Drew Sampson?"

A long pause. "What does any of this have to do with Drew?"

"He was involved with Celia."

"I think you'd better check your notes, Ms. Hayle." The nasty tone of her response surprised me; it seemed out of character.

"I have good reason to think otherwise. Do you happen to have a telephone number for him?"

A longer pause. "No. Is there anything else that I can help you with?"

"I'd like to talk to you again if I could."

My instincts told me she knew more than she was saying. It's always best to conduct an interview in person. If you know what to look for, only the best liar is able to conceal the truth. The gesture of a hand, the avoidance of eye contact, her posture in a chair, will give her away. You can find out more in ten minutes when you sit across from somebody than in ten hours on the phone.

"Well, I don't think that will be possible. I—"

"Please, Mrs. Donovan. The police are planning to open up the investigation again. I used to be in the department, and we PIs often share information with the authorities. With the cutbacks in the police force, it saves time and manpower. I suspect you might be more comfortable talking to me than to them."

"Could I ask who your client is?"

"I'm afraid I'm not at liberty to say."

"How did you get my name?"

"It was written in a book that belonged to Celia Jones, which I currently have in my possession," I said, implying that if she didn't talk to me I'd be inclined to turn said book over to the cops.

"And you're saying that if I talk to you I won't have to talk to the police?"

"I doubt very seriously if the police will contact you." Now *that* was the truth.

She sighed again. This is one sighing sister, I thought.

"Okay, but it will have to be soon. I'm leaving for my country home in Connecticut on Thursday night. I'll be there for the next few weeks. Maybe even until spring. I go there to find peace."

"Will tomorrow be okay?"

"No, Wednesday is better, and it will have to be early in the morning. Mornings are always best for me. Early morning. Eight o'clock."

I'm not a morning person, but I figured I'd better take what I could get. "Thank you. Before you hang up, I'd like Drew Sampson's telephone number if you have it," I asked her again, loading my request with the weight of pseudo-authority. My tone must have convinced her. She handed it over this time without question.

I smiled to myself. I'd counted on Rebecca Donovan not knowing squat about cops and private investigators, and the rules, hostilities, and occasional respect that mark our relationship. If she knew anything about law enforcement, she'd have known that most cops consider it beneath them to take a tip from a private investigator, and although PIs are law-abiding citizens, our first responsibility is *always* to our client. We work the same streets as the police, but from different directions. Most folks, though, would rather talk to a private investigator than a cop, particularly if the PI is a woman.

I wasn't so lucky with my next call.

"Who are you, how did you get my private number, and what do you want?" Drew Sampson had a squeak of a voice, the kind that might make a person laugh out loud if she didn't watch herself. I didn't remember him sounding like this in high school, but that had been a long time ago. He'd been such a handsome kid, nobody would have noticed it anyway.

"Good morning, Mr. Sampson. I'm a private investigator. Tamara Hayle of Hayle Investigative Services. I'd like to ask you a few questions, if I could."

"About what?"

"I'm looking into the death of a woman. If you have a moment, I think you may be able to clear things up for me."

"Why the hell are you calling me? And I'm asking you again, how did you get this number?"

"I got your number from Mrs. Clayton Donovan," I said, guessing correctly that the mention of Rebecca Donovan's name wrapped in her dead husband's mantle would win me a few minutes. He paused for a moment, which gave me time to throw in somebody else. "I also spoke recently with Larry Walton, and he said that it might be helpful for me to speak to you. Larry was extremely helpful, and he was certain that you'd be able to give me a bit of your time."

I hoped the double whammy of Rebecca Donovan and Larry Walton would do the trick; it almost did.

"So this woman is Celia Jones, I assume?"

"Yes. Celia Jones and her son, Cecil."

"I guess Larry told you about the grief that bitch and her little bastard caused me and my family, didn't he?"

"Actually, he just said I should talk to you," I said, recalling the adage about never telling everything you know. "If possible, I'd like to make an appointment to—"

"To what?"

"Well, to talk about your relationship with Celia Jones."

"That little whore got just what she deserved as far as I'm concerned and the same thing goes for her kid. I hope they both burn in hell."

That took me back a beat, but I quickly recovered. "Are the police aware of your feelings?" I asked in what I hoped was an appropriately threatening voice.

"Look, lady, you can tell the police, the Devil, or God himself what I said about that woman. I don't give a damn. As a matter of fact, I talked to the cops about her because of my wife's involvement with her—and I'll tell you what I told them: I was with a friend the day Celia Jones was murdered. It was New Year's Eve, and since we'd both had a lousy year, we thought we'd bring in the new year together. We got stinking drunk and both passed out on my couch. I didn't get up until three the next day. Now leave *me* the hell alone." He slammed down the phone so hard I could almost feel it. I placed the receiver back into the cradle, wondering what his wife had to say. I wasn't disappointed.

Annette Sampson made no bones about her eagerness to talk about her husband, Celia Jones, and what had happened between the three of them. We agreed to meet the next day, which was a Tuesday, at "high noon," as she said with a charming chuckle that indicated "high" was the operative word, which was fine with me. *In vino veritas* as they say. There is truth in wine. I was sure that Annette could give me the name of her husband's friend. He hadn't mentioned gender, and if he'd had something going on the side, I was sure she'd be more than willing to talk about it.

I was feeling pretty good by the end of the day. I'd jotted down verbatim what Rebecca, Drew, and Annette had said in my "redlocket" file, placing a star next to Drew Sampson's name. I was sure the cops hadn't pressed him hard. Their questions had probably been routine, and I doubted if they'd even bothered to check out his alibi. Drew Sampson was a big man in Newark. They wouldn't touch him unless they had him dead to rights. If they'd grilled anybody about Celia's death, it had probably been dumb, no-pot-to-piss-in Brent Liston.

But if they *did* have a case against Sampson, they wouldn't hesitate to bring him down, and I might be able to help them with that.

My advantage over the police was that I knew Celia Jones. I had her journal and knew what had been written in it. I would also have conducted face-to-face interviews with two women who looked like me, and I knew from experience they'd be more honest with me than they'd be with cops.

I couldn't make an arrest if I found out something important, but I could make it damn easy for the police to make one. I had a good contact in Griffin, and if push came to shove, there was always De-Lorca, my old boss from Belvington Heights. With a bit more digging, I might find out some crucial tidbit about the murder of Celia or her boy that had been overlooked, and the police would take the next step. Maybe then I'd be able to get a good night's sleep.

I've never seen anything like it. To shoot a woman right through her privates.

When it came to Celia's murder, I was sure that Old Man Morgan had called it right. Those bullets, shot at close range, had made a definite statement.

Fucking her was a very small part of our relationship.

How many other men—and women—could say the same?

I pulled out Celia's journal and looked again for something I might have missed, even though I was sure that her little red book had told me all it was going to tell. I called Aaron Dawson's number again, but it was disconnected. That would be one question Annette Sampson might be able to answer for me: Who the hell was Aaron Dawson?

I was convinced that whoever killed Celia killed her son, too, for something he knew about his mother's murder but didn't realize he knew. What scared me, though, was if the murderer knew that Cecil had talked to me, then maybe our conversation had contributed to his death.

At the thought of that, my fears about the man in the black coat came back strong; they started in my belly and worked themselves clear up to my heart, and when the phone rang, I almost jumped out of my chair.

"Tamara, this is Larry Walton. I wanted to apologize to you about the way I left you yesterday. I asked you to brunch and I should at least have had the decency to walk you back to your car." He ran his words together in one long sentence, which got my guard up.

"No harm done."

"Listen, I, uh, wanted to clarify something. I mentioned that I was down south visiting my daughter, right? Well, uh, I may have made a mistake. I was out with a friend on New Year's Eve and into the next day, when Celia was killed."

"And that friend was Drew Sampson." It hadn't taken Sampson long to call in his chips.

"Drew didn't do anything to Celia. You have to believe that."

"Because he was with you, right?" I didn't hide my disbelief.

"Listen, I just wanted to let you know what the deal is, okay? I'm sorry, Tamara," he said as if he meant it.

"Right, thanks for calling, Larry," I said, trying hard to make my voice sound neutral.

An alibi was an alibi, and, for whatever reason, he was willing to give one to Sampson. Despite the tension between us, I liked Larry Walton, and it saddened me to see him compromise himself like this. If it was a compromise. I called the number he'd given me in North

Carolina to check his story, but got an answering machine. I hung up without leaving a message. Since I wasn't a cop, what was I going to say? His ex-wife would probably think I was some jealous hoochie trying to get the goods on her ex-husband's whereabouts on New Year's Eve. Drew Sampson and Larry Walton were each other's alibi, and that was that. But in my book that made them both look suspicious.

A B C D

I had to laugh at myself when I imagined the response any cop worth his badge would give me if I trotted out Celia's scribbles and tried to tie them to one of these men. They'd laugh me clear out of the squad room. I closed her book and put it back in my safe.

Larry aka Chessman, Drew, Clayton Donovan, Annette, they were all respectable, responsible members of this community. Celia and her son were the outsiders, the uninvited guests who had disrupted everyone's lives.

I typed a few more notes into "redlocket," recording my impressions of the conversations I'd had with Donovan, the two Sampsons, and the alibi Larry Walton gave Drew Sampson. I turned off the computer, emptied my teacup, locked my office, and headed downstairs, glancing into the Beauty Biscuit, hoping Wyvetta was working late. I could do with some friendly talk and a shot of bourbon. But Wyvetta had gone, so I started toward the parking lot, my mind on what I was going to fix for dinner and whether or not Jamal had finished his homework.

I felt the bastard's hand on my shoulder even before he grabbed it good. Out of the corner of my eye, I spotted his woman, dressed all in black, watching us from that broken-down midnight blue car I'd seen so long ago.

Had it been a woman in that long black coat?

"You killed Celia, didn't you? I know you did it, and I'm going to prove it," I shouted out because I couldn't think of another damn thing to say, and figured this would be as good as anything else. That was another thing I learned early on: All a woman has in a situation like this is her nerve, and all she can do is go for broke. Liston tightened his grip on my arm so hard I thought he would break it.

"And you killed Cecil, too, didn't you? You stupid son of a bitch, you killed your own son!" I screamed, my voice shrill with outrage, like *I* was the one who had hold of his arm.

I figured the bastard would do one of two things: He'd either kill me on the spot or let me go. To my surprise, he didn't do either. He started to cry, which shocked the hell out of me.

"I didn't do nothing to hurt that boy," he wailed. "I loved that boy. I didn't do nothing to hurt him!"

It could have been guilt or it could have been grief. Or it could have been fear because I'd figured it out. I stood there with my mouth hanging open, not sure what I was going to do next, but then realized I was free. As his woman climbed out of the car, I backed away, keeping my eyes on both of them, like you do on a junkyard dog whose sight is fixed on your leg. I was trembling hard when I got into my car, and I shook like a mold of my grandma's grape Jell-O all the way home.

My *confrontation with Liston* had left me tense, and I was still uneasy the next morning, so I allowed myself some self-prescribed luxury. After I'd gotten Jamal off to school, I soaked for twenty minutes in a tub filled with bubbles, read a few chapters of a mystery, then made myself pancakes for breakfast. I took my good time getting to Annette Sampson's house. By the time I got there, it was "high noon," and the midday sun was pouring through the diamond-paned windows of her living room.

Her house, which was located on a narrow street in Belvington Heights, was modest, to put it kindly. When I was a cop in the Heights, I'd been surprised to learn that the town had unfashionable areas. For a kid growing up in the Hayes Homes in Newark, Belvington Heights represented the "height" of good taste and high living, offering the best of everything—best schools, best people, best homes. It never occurred to me that these highly paid people had poorly paid servants to do their bidding, and that the "help" were usually black and lived in these small, cramped houses.

Annette Sampson's house needed some serious work. A coat of

Benjamin Moore would have done it some good, and three coats would have done it better. The front porch sagged, and birds had built a nest in a corner of the roof. The lawn, if you could call it that, was mostly dirt, and winter had turned last summer's effort at a garden into mud. My place in East Orange, with all its faults, was in better shape. But location is everything in real estate, and if this house were put on the market it would have brought in big bucks. If it had been perched on certain streets in Newark, she couldn't have given it away.

"I grew up here. The house belonged to my father," Annette Sampson told me as we settled down on her couch, a yellow plastic number that would be hot as hell in the summer. The glass coffee table was chipped, and a leg on one of the chairs was missing. Old newspapers and magazines were strewn around the room like nobody gave a damn. It was hard to imagine this messy place housed the elegant woman in the stunning silk suit I'd seen at Morgan's on Saturday.

"My father was chauffeur/handyman for a rich pharmacist, who owned a string of drugstores, which is probably why I ended up marrying a pharmacist," she continued. "I know I need to put some money into this house, but money is something I don't have at this point. But it belongs to me. It's all *mine,* and that sure feels good." Her emphasis on "mine" clearly summed up her relationship with her husband.

She made a pitcher of Bloody Marys and poured the mixture into two remarkably pretty crystal glasses. Crackers and cheese were carelessly arranged on a matching platter, and I suspected the hastily thrown together snack was an excuse to serve the drinks. I took a sip of mine, which was heavy on the vodka, then held the glass up to examine it.

My family hadn't gone in much for fancy glassware. My father usually drank his liquor out of a mayonnaise jar, and the rest of us used whatever cheap, mismatched things my mother picked up from the sales table at the A&P. I didn't grow up seeing a lot of good crystal.

"I have only two of these beautiful glasses left," Annette said, noticing my interest. "My mother gave them to me as a wedding present. They're Steuben. Très expensive. I had six once, but I threw two at my ex-husband in a rage. Celia broke one, and I dropped the fourth on the way to the kitchen last week. These are the only two I have left. I never use them when I'm alone, I only use them when I have company, which is rare these days. When I'm alone, I drink out of a plain old, ugly water glass."

"A water glass?" I didn't hide my surprise, and she laughed at my response.

"These dainty little things don't hold enough booze if I want to get seriously drunk. But I like things to match when somebody visits me. I need to have order, and matching glasses and dishes keep me from feeling like my life has dissolved into chaos."

"I know what you mean," I said as if I did. Truth was, my life stayed in chaos, and all the matching glasses in the world wouldn't straighten it out. As a matter of fact, *nothing* in my kitchen matched. Not glasses, dishes, spoons, or forks, and I was too busy and broke to give a damn one way or the other.

"So you threw one at your husband? That's something I always wanted to do to my ex," I said. But if I'd aimed something at De-Wayne Curtis it would have been a damn sight deadlier than a glass.

"Actually he's not my ex yet. Despite everything that has happened between us, we haven't begun divorce proceedings."

"Is there any chance of reconciliation?"

Her answer was in the look she shot me as well as in her laughter, and I found myself laughing with her. Suddenly, I could see what Celia might have seen in her. She had a mischievous, seductive edge that broke through her tight middle-class veneer as subtly as the black lace teddy peeking from her white Gap blouse.

"So Celia broke one of your glasses, too?" I veered back to the reason for my visit. "How did that happen?"

"She didn't throw it at me, if that's what you're asking. Celia wasn't the type to throw things. I'm the type to throw things."

I took a nibble of cheese and a sip of my drink. She poured herself another one and raised it in a toast.

"To Celia," she said.

"To Celia."

She finished it off and dabbed her lips with one of the linen cocktail napkins on the tray. They, too, must have been left over from her former life.

"I've had enough," she said, which surprised me since she'd just pegged herself as a drunk, and I knew from life with father that drunks never got enough. She went into the kitchen, filled a glass with ice water, came back, and set it next to the one that had contained her drink. "I've been drinking too much these days," she confided as if we'd been friends for years.

"Then you'd better toss out those water glasses and get yourself some juice glasses instead," I suggested.

"You're probably right," she said with a good-natured smile.

"Maybe you're still grieving the loss of Celia," I offered, and she nodded that it was the truth.

"I know I have to stop drinking and get back to living, but it's harder than it sounds." She looked disconcerted for a moment, and I took the lull in our conversation to glance at the key words I'd scribbled in my notebook: Celia Jones, Drew Sampson, Rebecca Donovan, Aaron Dawson.

I rarely take notes during an interview. I have a good memory and if I've written down key words, I can always recall what was said. I decided to start with "Celia" and work my way down the list. I closed my book and dropped my pen back into my bag, as if the interview were over and we were just two women sitting around talking about nothing.

"You're right about Celia," I said. "She wasn't the type to throw things, even in high school."

She looked surprised. "So you knew Celia, too. I thought that you were simply involved with her case on a professional level."

"No, Celia and I were best friends in high school. We were inseparable."

"Funny, she never mentioned you, and she told me almost everything about her life." She was suspicious, and I remembered what Larry had said about how possessive she'd been.

"We grew apart over the years, but I still cared about her. I was very distressed to hear that she'd been murdered, particularly in the way it was done." I watched her closely, but there was no indication of feeling, not even grief.

"I loved her," she said after a moment or two with no change of expression. "And it was a complete surprise to me to fall in love with another woman. I don't think I'm a lesbian or anything. I mean, up until my affair with Celia, I always liked men, but I fell in love with her spirit, the thing that made her Celia, and that went beyond gender."

"And what made her Celia?" I asked because I had begun to wonder myself. Although Larry Walton said he hadn't been in love with Celia, his feelings ran deep. I wondered how the wild, young Celia I'd known could evoke such strong emotions from two such different people—and from the person who had shot her womb full of holes.

Annette shifted her attention to a drawing that hung on the wall, and my eyes followed hers. It was a drawing of Celia, but it was unfocused and vague. I wondered if this dreamy rendition represented her fantasy of Celia, or a lack of skill.

"Celia gave me everything I needed," she said quietly, as if she'd forgotten I was there. "I loved her because she made me aware of parts of myself that I didn't know I had. Knowing her made me more aware of myself. She gave me a sense of who I could be, what I could do. She was the light of my life."

As she spoke, memories of what Celia Jones had meant to me came back. Celia had always been the daring one, the one who called the shots, made everything seem simple and possible. Her impish, dare-you-to-try-it grin never failed to convince me to do forbidden, dangerous things, but it also prodded me to take risks I never would have taken on my own, and those risks often paid off. When we were girls, Celia's reckless spirit took root in my own and eventually gave me the strength to become the woman I am. Even though we'd parted ways, it was Celia's courage, coupled with the memory of my brother, that led me to become a cop, leave DeWayne Curtis, and start my own detective agency. Recalling Celia's passion for life made me smile, but that smile was shadowed by sorrow. How could my old friend have ended up like she had?

"I married young. My life basically belonged to my husband and son, and if you've met my husband, you know what that was like. I was a cliché, stay-at-home mom, rich husband, nothing in my life," Annette continued, drawing my attention back to her.

"A lot of women would envy that." My long hours and low finances often made me fantasize about some Prince Charming swooping down and taking care of me. What I'd seen of Drew Sampson, though, hinted that her "champagne and roses" life had been more like tap water and dandelions.

"What about your husband? Was he involved with somebody during your marriage or is he now?"

"Drew? Have you met him? All he cares about is his business."

"He must have been pretty angry when he found out about you and Celia?"

She laughed and rolled her eyes. "Pretty angry is putting it mildly. I've never known him to be so mad. He is still very bitter about it."

"Is there any chance—"

"That he killed Celia?" she said, not letting me finish. "Believe me, I've thought about it, and it scares the hell out of me. What people don't know about the great Drew Sampson is that he has an evil, violent temper that very few people see. I sure saw enough of it, though. He never hit me, but there was always the threat of it in his voice. He loves his son, I'll give him that, and he would do anything to protect him. I know he would never hurt Drew Junior. But I wouldn't put killing Celia or anybody else who he finds threatening beyond him."

"So you think he could have killed Celia?"

"Yeah. He could have done it."

I took her answer with a grain of salt. Ask half a dozen women that question about their ex-husbands, and they'd say the bastard is capable of anything. Yet I couldn't entirely dismiss her feelings. I wondered what Larry Walton would say if he heard them.

"So when Celia came into your life everything changed?"

"Not at first. I wasn't sure how I felt about her. She was kind of vulgar and crude. Not at all the kind of woman my mama would approve of."

I smiled to myself. Even as a kid, Celia had a sewer mouth and a collection of dirty jokes that could make my brother blush.

"How long were you and Celia together?"

"We had this, I guess you could say, flirtation about a year before we actually got together. I left my husband and Celia moved in here about a year ago. We broke up four months before she was killed."

"So how did you meet her?"

"Rebecca Donovan."

Now *that* surprised me. I took a sip of my drink and nibbled meditatively on a piece of cheese before I asked for more. "Mrs. Donovan mentioned that she was involved in a shelter for abused women. So you worked in the same shelter?"

"No, not at the shelter. Rebecca has always had a bit of the social worker about her."

I smiled to myself, remembering how Larry Walton had used nearly the same words to describe Annette's attitude toward Celia.

"I was in a show." She picked up the puzzled look on my face and gestured to the drawing of Celia I'd noticed earlier. "I like to draw. I'm an artist," she added with a defiant shrug as if daring me to contradict her, and I realized that this self-definition was probably one that she had only recently begun to use. "I haven't studied art formally or anything, but I've always loved to draw. My husband calls my efforts amateurish, and maybe they are, but I love to do it, and I know I'll improve. I'm determined to get better."

"Good for you," I said, and meant it. She spoke with a pride and self-assurance that reminded me of those times I'd defied all odds to accomplish what I wanted. Maybe Celia had given her that spirit, too.

"So you and Rebecca Donovan are good friends?"

"Yeah, after all these years. As a matter of fact, we still get together, usually at the beginning of the month. An early breakfast usually. We always see each other on holidays, too, like Thanksgiving or Christmas, or we call from wherever we are. Always early, when everybody else is in bed. It's an old tradition. We were kind of like sisters when we were young because we were both only children. When we were kids we had to get up to go to sunrise service. And they meant sunrise."

"Sunrise!" My voice betrayed my penchant for late mornings.

Annette laughed. "Yeah, sunrise! Becky and I go back, way back. Our parents belonged to the same church." She gave an exaggerated shiver and picked up the drink she'd sworn off a few moments earlier.

"I take it you're no longer a member."

"You don't miss a trick, do you, Ms. Hayle?" she said with a grin. "That place, and a couple of other things, probably drove me to drink. I doubt if Becky is still a member, but she is always so rigid, maybe she still is. Becky took everything much more to heart than I did. I used to call her the little nun, because she had such a firm notion of good and evil and that people should always get their just deserts."

"Just desserts? That means peach cobbler to me."

"I'm with you, but Becky was serious about justice. Maybe that's why she married a judge."

"So what was your church like?"

"When I think back about it, it was more a cult than a church. Services three and four times a week. All day in church and meetings afterward. Maybe it had more of an influence on both of us than we realize. Negative on me, maybe that was why I ended up in a 'sinful' relationship with Celia. God knows, I would have ended up in hell for that one. But all the good works that Becky did may have come from that, too. She was always doing something good for somebody, which is why she got involved in Celia's life in the first place, and how I met her.

"She came to the show because she wanted to support me in my art, and brought Celia to expose her to the quote better things in life."

"You said you didn't like her at first."

Annette glanced at the drawing of Celia, then twisted her mouth into a half smile that broke into a full grin. "Maybe that's too harsh. It wasn't so much that she was vulgar, but she said exactly what was on her mind. She didn't like any of the art in the show and made no bones about it, rather loudly I might add. She was like, what the hell is this shit?"

"But she liked your work?"

"No, not particularly. She liked me. I think she was more drawn to me than I was to her, and she made it her business to get to know me better."

"So what did Mrs. Donovan, the little nun, I think you called her, think about that?"

"I think it surprised her, but Rebecca has one of those faces that never gives anything away. It's impossible to know what she really feels or even if she's happy or sad."

"What do you mean?"

"A couple of years back, Becky lost a child, only a few weeks old. Crib death, I think it was. She really wanted kids, and it was the saddest thing in the world, but she wouldn't let anyone share her grief. I'm sure that she and the judge mourned the death of their child in private, but never in front of anybody else."

Annette's sigh evoked a similar one from me. We were both mothers so we knew how deep this woman's pain must have been. I couldn't imagine my life without my son; I didn't want to imagine it.

"And her husband died before they could have another child?" I asked, my attention leaving Annette for a moment to focus on what had happened to her friend.

"There must have been some kind of a problem because she couldn't conceive again. But if you saw her to talk to you'd never know it." She grunted in disgust. "That was part of our church's teaching, too. The Lord has His reasons, so you can't question His ways. To show sorrow was to doubt His will and challenge His wis-

dom. Beats the hell out of me, too," she said irreverently, acknowledging my confusion. "How Rebecca ended up with Clay Donovan is
one of the great mysteries of life."

"I hear he was a wild one," I said with a salacious grin, hoping to
dig up more dirt on the judge, but if she knew anything she wasn't
about to share it. She simply gave a devil-may-care shrug and gulped
more of her drink, the water apparently abandoned.

"So who is Aaron Dawson?" I had saved the best for last.

"The man Celia left me for." If she felt any bitterness she didn't
show it.

"And you weren't angry about it?"

"Of course I was angry, and I told someone I love some very hurt-
ful, very destructive things that I shouldn't have shared because of
what happened and what she did to me. But I got over it."

"What did you tell?"

"It's done now. It's over. I don't want to repeat it."

But she took in her breath suddenly, as if she had just remembered something, and then she glanced once at the drawing on the
wall and then away from me. I wondered what had come into her
mind.

"So why did Celia leave?"

"Because she was pregnant."

Through her womb, the center of a woman's being.

I was the one concealing my feelings now, and it took some serious willpower to do it.

"Celia was a stupid cunt when it came to men." The use of the
"c" word casually spilling out of the mouth of this supposedly well-

bred woman sent a shiver of disgust through me, but I hid my feel-ings as she continued her rant.

"Half the time she screwed them and didn't use a rubber. Liked it raw, she used to say. Can you imagine that! That's the kind of thing some low-life man says to a woman, not the other way around! She could have caught anything, brought it back home to me, anything at all. She could be a dumb little cunt when she felt like it. A real dumb bitch." The anger poured out in her voice, in the tight line her lips formed, and the fury in her eyes. Celia had been dead for nearly four months, but the rage was still there, and it had finally broken through.

"What a terrible betrayal! Celia could definitely be a bitch." I hid my feelings and threw in my two cents' worth as I remembered the dust from that midnight blue Lincoln the last time I saw her. "So she was pregnant when she was murdered?" I wondered why Morgan hadn't bothered to mention it. Perhaps old-fashioned tact had kept his lips sealed; "Bury the secrets of the dead with them" had always been his motto.

"I don't know." Annette shrugged as if she didn't give a damn one way or the other.

"Is Aaron Dawson the kind of man who would kill a woman over having—or not having—his baby?"

"Why don't you ask him," she said sharply. She began to collect the things that were on the coffee table, the tray, pitcher, and glasses, and headed into the kitchen with them, her not-so-subtle way of in-dicating that our interview was over.

But I wasn't ready to go, and I followed her, notebook in hand.

"Do you know where he lives or how I can get in touch with him? The numbers I have are disconnected."

She made me wait while she carefully washed and dried her pretty crystal glasses and climbed on a footstool to place them next to each other on the top shelf.

"Cecil knew his number. After Celia died he stayed with him for a while, but Cecil is dead now, too, so I guess you're out of luck." Her caustic tone surprised me because it came from nowhere. But I didn't have a chance to respond. Our attention was drawn to the sound of a key turning in the kitchen door lock.

"Drew?" Annette called out climbing down from the footstool.

"Yeah."

"Drew, where have you been?"

"Don't ask me that, and I told you what my name is! My name is DeeEss. Call me that or nothing. I came to get the keys." He held his small body tight, his shoulders scrunched up close to his neck. He lifted a set of car keys off a hook near the kitchen door and jiggled them defiantly.

There was a snicker behind him as Pik, dressed in the usual gangsta regalia, sauntered into the room. The young woman I had seen at Morgan's stood behind him, as if she were afraid to enter. She held her baby, who started to giggle, adding an odd note of levity to a tense situation. The girl kissed the child's forehead and cheek.

Pik picked an apple up from a wooden bowl on the table, took a bite, then tossed the remainder into a nearby trash can as if shooting for a basket. I glanced at Annette, who was clearly afraid of him. I was tempted to call him on his manners, but was caught between instinct and common sense. Scolding a strange kid these days can earn you a bullet through the head as quickly as a tongue stuck out behind your back. But this boy irked me. He had this woman cowering in her own kitchen, and I didn't like it.

"I'm Ms. Tamara Hayle," I said, looking the kid in the eye. "I saw you at my godson's funeral." The godson business was a stretch, but in different circumstances it might have been so. I stuck out my hand toward Pik in a gesture of friendliness. He stared at it for a few moments then shoved his into his pockets. I was lucky he didn't spit in it.

The baby started to giggle again, and I turned to the girl.

"Cristal, isn't it?"

"Yes, ma'am," she said, and her politeness surprised me.

"That's a beautiful baby. Can I hold her?"

"Him. He a boy," said Pik, and both of us glanced at him. I reached toward the baby and Pik moved in front of her, preventing me from taking him.

"Cecil didn't have no godmother," he said.

"Goes to show you, Pik, there's a lot of stuff about Cecil Jones you don't know."

He gave me what he thought was a scary look, but I've taken on scarier thugs than him, so I didn't flinch.

"I'm DeeEss," said Annette's son, who apparently had enough regard for his mother to try to keep a bad scene from exploding in her kitchen.

"Tamara Hayle." I shook his hand, which was as soft and delicate as a girl's. I thought again about what Larry Walton had said about Annette and her son, and how selfish she had been to drag her son into her new life. She had gambled everything on Celia Jones and lost, big-time.

"Are you Jamal's mother? I think he might have been in my home-room in fifth grade. I think I remember you."

"Yes, I am."

"How's Jamal doing?"

"Fine. He's doing just fine. I'll tell him you asked about him," I said, which was a lie.

But for a moment, I glimpsed DeeEss as he must have been be-fore Celia and her child entered his life. He was a kid who had been a friend of my son's, and my heart broke for him and his mother. Pik caught a glimpse of that boy, too, and didn't like what he saw.

"Let's hat, man," he gestured toward the door, and without a word to either me or Annette, the three of them left. I heard some-body gunning the engine of Annette's car before they pulled away.

Annette fell down on her knees. "Oh Lord, please, Lord, don't let what happened to Celia's boy happen to mine. Please, Lord, please please," she cried into her folded hands, praying like she must have at those sunrise services her parents dragged her to.

"I'm certain he'll be fine," I said, reassuring her, but I wasn't so sure. Trouble usually finds boys like hers like lint finds black velvet. "If you need me or think of anything else, please call me," I said, placing my card with my cell phone number into her folded hands. When I left I closed the door behind me, but I don't think she heard a thing.

The homes of the two old friends couldn't have been more different. Rebecca Donovan's house, with its well-tended yard and beautiful exterior, was a candidate for a spread in *Better Homes and Gardens*. She didn't live in the Heights, but in a stately neighborhood in Newark, where out of loyalty and love for the city, many professionals and politicians chose to reside. In the old days, homes like these, with their wide porches and stately cupolas, could be found in many Newark neighborhoods. But they'd fallen on hard times; most now were stuffed with too many families.

As I drove down Rebecca Donovan's street, I was proud of how beautifully the neighborhood had been preserved and pleased to claim it for my city. It was like those streets I remembered driving down with my father when I was a kid. On Sundays, my father would take us picnicking on the lake in Weequahic Park, and we'd end up at the Dairy Queen on Ferry Street for cherry vanilla ice cream cones. Come spring, we'd stroll through Branch Brook Park, where the homegrown cherry blossoms challenged—and whipped—those in DC. Weequahic, Chancellor Avenue. Lyons Avenue. I could still hear the names of those grand old places rolling off my father's lips. Someday they would be back to what they were; I hoped I'd be around to see it.

The Donovan house was located across from the park. It was a red brick Dutch Colonial, with a circular driveway and an impressive front lawn that whispered class. As I parked my car, I caught a glimpse of the spacious backyard with flower beds that probably bloomed with tulips and impatiens in spring. A white picket fence strung with climbing vines, roses I'd bet, surrounded the yard. It was the kind of backyard kids dream about, particularly if they grow up in the projects like I did. I remembered what Annette had told me about Rebecca Donovan and got sad for her all over again. Here she had a big old house, planned for a big old family, and everything she had dreamed about had been snatched away. I thought about my own son then, as I always do in these situations, and gave a quick prayer of thanks for my good fortune. My mind was still on Jamal when Rebecca Donovan opened the front door.

Her eyes were what struck me first. They were brown and as soft as a puppy's, but the sorrow in them revealed her grief. Yet she had the quick smile of a little girl, which lit up her face and brought a smile to mine. Her hair was streaked with gray and pulled into a bun at the nape of her neck, which made me recall Annette's nickname for her. Her pretty skin, the color of unshelled walnuts, was dotted here and there with freckles.

"Come in, Ms. Hayle. I'm an early bird. My husband didn't come into his own until noon. Since his death I've reverted to my own ways," she greeted me when she opened the door. I was struck by her warmth and how different she seemed from the woman I'd spoken to on the phone two days ago. The mention of her late husband so early in our conversation also surprised me, but he'd been dead only since the end of August, less than a year. She was still mourning him, and would be for a long time.

She was dressed in stylish earth-brown wool pants and a neat, rust-colored silk blouse. Tasteful gold stud earrings peeked from her ears and a thin gold chain graced her neck. In her casual way, Rebecca Donovan was as elegant and understated as her classy home. She too could have stepped from a magazine on upscale, suburban living.

"Thank you so much," I said, suddenly conscious of my lint-covered black wool coat, which I keep forgetting to take to the cleaners. I'd meant to wear my good one, but it was the first thing I grabbed when I stumbled out of my house at what seemed like the crack of dawn.

"I hope it's not too early for you."

"No, it's fine. It does my soul good to get moving early," I said, lying. I enjoyed getting up this early in the morning about as much as a toothache. But it was a clear, bright winter's day and once I got going, I felt virtuous.

"Would you like some coffee?"

"No, thanks, I've had my quota for the day." And wouldn't have made it this far if I hadn't, I said to myself.

"You don't mind if I have some, do you? I thought we could talk in the sunroom. On a morning like this it's so cheerful and warm in there. It used to be our favorite room, mine and Clayton's. On snowy weekends, Clayton would build a fire, and we'd just sit there in front of it and chat clear into evening." Her eyes had filled with tears and she turned her head to hide them. "Please, make yourself comfortable. I'll only be a moment." She nodded toward a room that adjoined the well-appointed living room and I headed toward it.

I was taken aback when I entered it. The room was a shrine to her late husband. Awards and plaques from countless clubs and civic organizations filled the bookcases, many stacked against one another at odd angles. Large photographs of him alone and them as a couple covered every conceivable space. Birthday and anniversary cards and thank-you notes were tucked in front of books and on the table.

I understand grief. I understand the anger it brings, and how it can drive you crazy. I understand how far you must go into it in order to come out on the other side, and the wild places your mind will take you. Yet I was overwhelmed by the depth of this woman's pain.

Walking around the cozy room, I randomly picked up items, fascinated by the life that had been preserved—his pipes, toy models of his Porsche and motorcycle, mugs, cups, and plates with his name stenciled in fancy lettering. One that said "Here Come Da Judge" brought my last conversation with Jake to mind and made me smile.

A bar in the corner of the room covered with glasses stacked next to liquor bottles looked ready for service, and a bottle of Balvenie Portwood Scotch drew my attention. My brother Johnny used to call this twenty-one-year-old Scotch "a whiskey lover's poison." He drank Johnnie Walker Red, but liked the good stuff—and *this* was the good stuff—when he could get it. It was what I always gave him for his birthday. It was what he was drinking the night he put his gun in his mouth.

On the top shelf of a small bookcase was a black porcelain vase with a golden lid, which caught the morning sun and gleamed as if it had just been polished. It was a beautiful vase; I'd never seen one quite like it.

"I see you're admiring my vase. Actually it's an urn now, which contains my husband's ashes," Rebecca said, as she entered the room with a silver tray loaded with coffee, cream, sugar, and two dainty china cups. "Clayton brought it back from a trip to Japan. He loved it so much, I thought it would be fitting."

"Did he collect ceramics?"

"No, he just saw that vase and fell in love with it. If Clayton collected anything it was liquor," she added with a nod toward the bar and a chuckle. "I rarely touch it, that's why there is so much of it left. I only drink when somebody insists that I join them. Nobody ever had to force my Clayton, though. He was a serious drinker. He liked good Scotch and good times." She put the tray down on the coffee table in front of the brown leather couch.

"That's what Clayton always told me. He'd say, 'Baby, this is what I want out of life—good times and good Scotch, and good loving from you.' He'd always add that when I cocked my eyebrow to remind him." She chuckled at the memory as we sat down. It was a luxurious couch, deep, soft, and made for someone who liked comfort and didn't mind paying for it.

"Yes, my late brother liked Scotch, too," I said, trying to put my thoughts about my brother out of my mind, but they were always there, lurking in the corners. Rebecca Donovan's loss was far more recent than mine, and my heart broke for her. Sitting with this woman and the grief she still carried, I suddenly felt that those key words I'd jotted down in my notebook were irrelevant.

"Whenever Judge Donovan's name comes up, everyone says

what a remarkable man he was and what a loss his death was to Newark. I'm so sorry I never had a chance to meet him."

That made her smile, but her eyes brimmed with tears again.

"Why don't you join me? One more cup won't hurt."

"The last time I started off the morning with too much coffee on an empty stomach, I turned into a gorilla," I said, remembering my hopped-up conversation with Larry Walton.

"Would you like something to eat?"

"Oh no, I'm fine. Actually, I did have some cereal this morning, so maybe I will have a cup," I said, quickly letting her know that I wasn't angling for a meal. She poured two cups of coffee and sank back into the couch.

"You would have liked my husband. Most women did. We were older when we married, and I felt lucky to get him. Not a morning goes by that I don't expect him to come dashing in at dawn, after a late night out with his boys looking for a midnight snack when all I want to do is sleep." She shook her head, as if still scolding him.

I tactfully glanced away and sipped my coffee, thankful I had it. From what Jake said, those late nights out usually involved the other gender.

"His death shook up so many people," I said, stating Jake's repeatable comment.

"Yes. But in a way, it was almost predictable."

Her response surprised me. "Why do you say that?"

"My husband loved to take chances. He was a daredevil and a half. He loved the thrill of living on the edge. I'm not sure what he saw in me, because I'm so very different."

"Opposites attract!" I volunteered the old cliché, and she nodded in agreement.

"If he'd been a more cautious man, he would have heeded the signs that his body was giving him. People die of walking pneumonia because they don't pay attention to their health until it's too late. You've got to listen to your body, slow down, take it easy, rest your bones when you're sick. Clayton was like a fireball. Nothing would stop him, not even an illness that turned deadly so quickly.

"He wouldn't rest. He wouldn't see a doctor. There was always somewhere to go, someplace to ride or late night appointment to keep, and before he knew it his lungs had filled with so much fluid he couldn't breathe. He was wheezing and coughing so hard I thought his body would break. I rushed him to the emergency room, but it was too late."

I was sorry I'd made her relive her husband's death. I remembered Annette's words about her not revealing her true feelings, but as far as I could tell, she had shared them with me. I knew from experience that it's often easier to unburden yourself to a stranger than a friend. Folks have told me unbelievably personal stories on late night flights or long train rides. The kindness of strangers has comforted me more often than I care to remember, and I was glad to play that role for her.

"The terrible irony was that I'd had a very serious and painful medical emergency of my own a few months before, and he'd brought me to the same hospital, the same cubicle even. I never want to see that place again," she added with a shudder and I nodded that I understood.

Neither of us spoke for a while. I placed my notebook down on the coffee table, and she added more cream to her cup.

"I'm sorry to burden you with this," she said after a moment. "I know you didn't come here to listen to my sad story."

"No, it's really okay. How are you doing now?"

She smiled slightly. "Not too great. I have a terrible time sleeping at night, so my doctor prescribed a very strong sedative. But I don't like to take sleeping pills, so I haven't even bothered to open the bottle. You can't take drugs forever. Sooner or later you have to face reality, and do the things that will make reality more acceptable, things that make it easier for you to get through your life. You need to find some kind of final resolution, one that will give you peace at last."

"Yes, that's true. Sometimes, I find it hard to sleep, too," I said, desperate to share something about myself, and draw her away from this painful subject. "And when I wake up, the look on my son's face tells me that my rest was not exactly restorative."

We both laughed a little at that and she asked, "You have a son?"

"Yes. Jamal. He's growing up faster than I ever thought he could. One moment you're nursing them and the next—" I stopped midsentence when I noticed her anguished expression. Here I'd gone and raked up another tragic memory for the woman. "I'm sorry," I stammered.

"I see you've talked to Annette, and she's told you what happened to my little boy."

"Yes. I saw her yesterday."

Her lips drew into a thin, sad smile. "Another irony in my life. Clayton died on the last day in August. Our baby died the same day, but three years earlier. I don't know what I'll do this year when that day rolls around again. I had Clayton to help me get through it before. Now—" She paused and then continued. "I named him after his father. Clayton Donovan Junior. He was so pleased to have a son."

When somebody shares that kind of sorrow, it's hard to know what to say. If you know them well, you ease their sadness with a hug or touch, otherwise you try to come up with words you hope will be healing, which was what I tried to do.

"Mrs. Donovan, you've given so many gifts to so many people. You've changed and enhanced so many lives, and I'm sure you will continue to do that. I'm sure your husband knew how fortunate he was to have you in his life. Your friend Annette Sampson certainly does. She has such respect and love for you, too."

"Annette and I were girls together, and somehow we've managed to maintain a friendship, even though she's done a great many things I don't approve of." Her tone was remarkably judgmental, and I was reminded momentarily of the old "church lady" routine Dana Carvey used to do on *Saturday Night Live*. But then she chuckled, and the warmth came back into her eyes. "Annette is my friend, despite her selfish, immoral blunders."

"I take it you're referring to Celia Jones."

"Yes. Miss Celia Jones." A pained look, a grimace really, settled on her face and she gulped her coffee down hard, as if washing Celia down with it. "Did you know Miss Celia Jones?"

It was odd the way she phrased it, spitting out Celia's name. The bond between us was suddenly broken; the mere mention of the possibility of a relationship with Celia had snapped it. She was the aloof, proper lady again, the one I'd spoken to on the phone. But in a way, I was relieved. We were back on a professional level, and I could ask blunt questions more honestly.

"She was my best friend in high school."

"I hope she was a better friend to you than she was to many others."

"I hadn't seen her in years."

"That was wise on your part."

"You mentioned before that you met her at a women's shelter?" I said, eager to go back to why I'd come.

"Yes."

"I understand that you introduced Celia to Annette Sampson."

"Yes, I did."

"I sensed that Mrs. Sampson was very bitter over the fact that Celia left her. Was she angry because you introduced her?"

"No. We still have our breakfasts. Annette didn't blame me. My regret is bringing Celia Jones into all of our lives, but I was just trying to do the right thing. How could I possibly know it would end up like this." She shook her head slowly, as if still trying to fathom the unraveling of her friend's life.

"I'm curious about Brent Liston. You stated when we spoke before that the judge had helped Celia escape from him?"

I couldn't tell exactly what aspect of her face changed. Was it her eyes that widened slightly or her lower lip that hardened into a pout? Something was altered. I wondered if it was the mention again of her husband or had it been the thought of Brent Liston.

"It's pretty simple really," she said, her tone belied what showed on her face. "I took Celia to meet Clayton, and he was very kind to her. I think he felt very sorry for her because he did everything he could to make things easier for her. I found out after he died that he had even given her some money; he was that kind of man. He put away Liston to help her feel safe. Liston had just gotten out, but both Clayton and I agreed that she should be protected from him, so he put him away for a while to protect her and her son."

I got an eerie feeling in my bones and suddenly I was afraid for her, living alone as she did in this big house.

"Has Brent Liston ever threatened you?"

"No."

"You mentioned before that you're going out of town tomorrow. To Connecticut, I think you said. Will you be safe there?"

She smiled, trying to put me at ease. "I feel very safe there. It's isolated, but I like it that way, and I can take care of myself. Thanks so much for your concern, Ms. Hayle. Can I call you Tamara? I've shared so much of myself with you, I feel as if I know you. Please call me Rebecca."

"Okay. Thanks. Tamara is fine. Where in Connecticut are you going?"

"About half an hour out of Hartford in a small town called Ashton. It's a lovely old town founded in the 1700s, mostly woods and farmland. Clayton and I fell in love with the place the moment we saw it. Maybe you and your son would like to visit me someday."

"I'd love to," I said but couldn't picture Jamal sitting happily in a house in the woods with two middle-aged women for more than fifteen minutes. "Is it hard to find?"

"Not if you know where to look. The town is very small, and everybody knows everybody else. We're the only black people who've bought there, so you can literally ask anybody in town—any gas station or convenience store attendant—where Judge Donovan lives, and they can tell you."

"Do you ever feel vulnerable, like if some criminal wanted to get even with the judge, he'd know where to find him?" I thought again of Brent Liston.

"It doesn't worry me, but I think it must have occurred to Clayton. He doesn't like guns, but he kept several there, and he showed me how to use them."

"Probably a good idea. It must be great to have a country home. Most folks I know considered themselves lucky to have the one they live in."

"It's fun during the summer. We used to have friends visit us all the time. Larry Walton came up regularly with his wife and daughter when they were together, and Annette and Drew spent many weekends with us. I like to go there in the winter now. I love to see the leaves change in October, and that first snowfall. Clayton is always with me."

She began to gather up the coffee items, placing them back on the tray, and I recalled Annette Sampson's hint that it was time for me to go. But yesterday's tension was absent today. I admired this woman's quiet dignity and suddenly cared a great deal about her welfare.

"I have one more question," I said.

"Sure. What is it?"

"Why did you go to Celia's funeral, Rebecca?"

"Because it was the proper thing to do," she said quietly, and after we had shared our thoughts about loneliness, insomnia, and the virtues of good coffee, I left Rebecca Donovan to her memories and headed back to my office.

I t *was going on noon* when I left Rebecca Donovan, so I picked up some lunch and the *Star-Ledger* on the way back to my office and made another attempt to contact Aaron Dawson. His phone was still disconnected, so I settled down to enjoy my tuna on rye, Diet Coke, and whole-wheat doughnut picked up as a special treat from the Dunkin' Donuts on Central Avenue.

Although Rebecca Donovan hadn't told me anything new, I was sure she'd turn out to be a valuable resource. Even though the mere mention of Celia's name had set the woman's teeth on edge, there hadn't been the passionate response I'd gotten from others. Whether people loved or hated the girl, they seemed to do it with all their heart.

I rarely read the business section, but I did today and was rewarded for my effort with an article about Drew Sampson under the heading "Home-Grown Businessman Makes Good." The story gave a brief history of Sampson's life and told how he'd inherited a single drugstore from his father and turned it into a thriving small chain by the time he was forty. According to the article, he'd made a killing when he sold his business, and was looking forward to retiring and traveling to places "far and unknown." He was eager to spend quality time with his family, the article observed, because over the years he felt he'd neglected them and wanted to make up for lost time. I sucked my teeth in disgust when I read that.

The article also said that Sampson was a "model" citizen who "gave back" to the community and was proud to have grown up in Newark. There was a blurb at the bottom of the story announcing his lunchtime appearance at the Businessman's Club to which the public was welcome; the fifty-dollar price tag could be written off because the proceeds would go to charity.

I glanced at my watch. It was almost 12:30. If I hurried, I'd be able to pay my fifty bucks and catch him at the club. Although I hated spending money on lunch when I'd already eaten, I knew I couldn't miss the opportunity to confront Sampson in person. I had no idea what I was going to say, but at least I'd have a chance to observe him and maybe get a reaction out of him that might be helpful. It was clear that he wasn't going to give me an interview, so this would be the best I could do. Surprise is always an essential element when you want to pry the truth out of somebody, especially if you ambush him in a public place.

I'd worn my good gray suit for my interview with Rebecca Donovan, and luckily taken off my jacket when I gobbled down my lunch so the mayonnaise that found its way to the front of my blouse missed the lapel. Fortunately, I keep a paisley silk scarf along with a spare pair of heels and a decent-looking pocketbook in my file cabinet for such emergencies. I tied the scarf jauntily around my neck, successfully concealing the stain, dumped the contents of my trusty

Kenya bag into my leather handbag, and squeezed my feet into a pair of stylish heels. I ducked into the ladies' room down the hall for a quick self-appraisal and figured I looked professional enough to walk into the club without arousing suspicion, especially if I folded my coat so the lint wouldn't show and checked it at the door.

The Businessman's Club is tucked away on a side street off Broad. It's been around for the last few decades, managing to avoid the devastation that followed the riots in the 1960s, just in time to hold its head high during the 1990s in the "renaissance" that now marks the city. In the old days, most of the members were white, but now there are nearly as many black and Latino faces. Club members have played an important role in the rebuilding of Newark, even though the vast majority of them live in the affluent suburbs, and until recently wouldn't be caught dead in the city after dark, but the opening of the New Jersey Performing Arts Center and the presence of the new baseball team, the Newark Bears, changed all that. The "Club," as it's called by insiders, was and continues to be *the* civic organization to belong to, even though membership cost more than I make in six months.

It didn't surprise me that Drew Sampson was a member, and I'd read somewhere that Larry Walton had been inducted, too. I also recalled seeing a plaque from the club in the Donovan sunroom, so they counted the late judge among the membership. Jake had been invited to join, but declined the honor. He said he didn't completely trust the city's powers-that-be and was uncomfortable mixing and mingling with them.

As I walked into the club, I tried to maintain an air of self-confidence, but my "good" shoes had tightened around my feet like vises, making a graceful entrance impossible. I stumbled into the foyer like a drunk, then stood in awe of my surroundings. It was an old building that had been renovated to reflect the power of its members. The place was lit by chandeliers, and the mahogany walls and heavy velvet draperies kept sunlight to a minimum. The room was cavernous but divided into nooks and crannies designed for clandestine meetings and lucrative business deals. The air vibrated with testosterone. A maître d' dressed in a maroon uniform that matched the draperies stopped me when I entered.

"The lunch has begun, ma'am," he said with a glare, as if he'd caught me swiping rolls from a serving tray.

"I'm so sorry, but I was held up in an important meeting," I whispered back.

"I'm afraid the remaining tickets are for members and guests only."

"Actually, I'm meeting one of your members, Larry Walton," I said, taking a gamble, which considering the tone of our last conversation, was cheeky as hell. The manager hesitated for a moment and then led me to a chair in the back of the room.

"I'm afraid you'll have to sit here for the time being. Mr. Walton is seated in the front. I'd rather not interrupt the lecture."

"Thank you very much," I said as I settled into my seat.

As I glanced around the club, my lips curled in disgust; this place certainly lived up to its name. The only other women present were either waiting on tables or brought by their bosses as table decoration. By all rights, my friends Annie and Wyvetta, who both own small businesses, should have been members, but neither had ever been invited to join.

Larry Walton was seated near the podium as the maître d' had mentioned, and his attention, like that of everybody else, was fixed on Drew Sampson, who, I assumed by the rapt attention of the audience, was sharing vital advice on small businesses. But my small business had about as much in common with his as I did with the men who surrounded me. It was a big deal for me to pay my public service bill every month, and there were no potential buyers for Hayle Investigative Services anywhere on the horizon. I tuned out most of what he was saying and focused my attention on him.

He had the straight black hair and caramel-colored complexion of a South American expatriate, which made me recall Larry's comments about his Cuban grandmother. He wore an obviously expensive pin-striped suit with predictable trimmings—gold cuff links, conservative tie, black wing-tipped shoes—but his cocky manner and delivery was irritating. I remembered his rudeness on the phone and hoped he wouldn't curse me out when I approached him, even though in this rarefied world he'd probably watch what he said.

My ears perked up when he mentioned his travel plans. He repeated what had been reported in the newspaper about his desire to visit countries "far and unknown" adding a comment on his "curiosity" about distant kin he'd never met. He further emphasized the importance of connecting with his "roots" and how his "killing" would make it possible. I recalled his wife's comments about him being capable of murdering Celia, and the mention of "killing" and the grin on his face when he said it, made my skin crawl. His emphasis on family connections sounded as if he were preparing to move to Cuba, where he could live out his days untroubled by the American justice system. I've dealt with enough murderers to know that their violent actions often go hand in hand with their arrogance, and Drew Sampson struck me as just cocky enough to be publicly flaunting getting away with murder. Sampson wound up his talk with an appeal to all those who loved our "fair city," as he called Newark, to support it in as many ways as they could.

The room gave him a standing ovation, and I headed with the rest of the crowd to the front of the room to offer congratulations. Drew Sampson obviously had no idea that I was the annoying PI who had called him earlier in the week, so I was embraced by the warmth of his phony smile along with everybody else. I tried to linger near the edge of the crowd waiting for it to thin out. Unfortunately, I was spotted by Larry Walton, as he made his way to the exit.

"Tamara Hayle, what are you doing here?" He was clearly puzzled by my presence.

"Well, you know, Larry, I'm a small businessperson, just like you and everybody else, and I wanted to learn how to make my business grow," I stuttered, flashing what I hoped was a convincing grin.

"You're not here to—"

"Cause trouble? No, of course not!" I said, anticipating his question. "I just want to say a few words to Mr. Sampson. Can I call you later?"

He hesitated for a moment. "A few words like what?"

"My feelings about his interesting presentation," I said. "Can I call you?"

He looked doubtful. "Sure. I'm glad you're not still mad at me about the other night."

"Mad about the other night? Oh, no. Of course not! It's completely forgotten."

He looked relieved. "I'll talk to you later then?"

"Later!" I said, praying that the guest of honor hadn't heard Larry say my name.

Grinning all the way, I edged closer to Sampson, falling in step with the admirers who had gathered to hear his sage advice. As the only woman in the crowd, I immediately caught his eye, and he gave me that self-important, condescending smile that "successful" men bestow on women in these situations. I smiled back coyly.

"Well, miss. How can I be of help to you?" His high-pitched voice oozed charm.

"I just have a couple of questions for you. Is this a good time?" I added a cute shoulder twitch that suggested I might be up for some fun and games later if he wanted to wait around.

"Sure, miss. Now's as good a time as any." He nodded benevolently.

"Did you kill Celia Jones?" I asked, the grin still on my face.

Confusion filled his eyes. "What did you say?"

"I said, did you kill Celia Jones?"

The color drained from his face, and a hush went through the surrounding crowd. Still grinning like a fool, I kept my eyes glued on him. "Mr. Sampson, the cops didn't grill you like they should have, and somebody has to. You had reason to kill Celia Jones, and she was my friend. Now I'm asking you the question again, did you murder Celia Jones?"

I didn't really expect an answer and got what I expected. He'd been pale before, now his face turned as red as a strawberry. For one awful moment, I thought he was going to hit me, and the thought must have occurred to him, too, because he raised his hand and *that* look came into his eyes. He must have thought better of it, though, because he dropped his hand down to his side, but his fingers beat an impatient rhythm on his pin-striped leg.

"Who the fuck let this woman in here?" he said to nobody in particular, all the veneer of the classy businessman dripping away with the "f" word. It didn't seem to bother him, though, because he said it again. "I asked you people, who the fuck let this bitch in here, somebody get her the fuck out of here."

People moved away from me so fast you'd have thought I'd pulled out an AK-47. I didn't give a damn, though; I stayed right in his face.

"And why did you bother to go to Celia's funeral after what you did? Why were you there when you hated her like you did? It was guilt, wasn't it? You're damned guilty!"

He stepped toward me, the only person who dared. I took a step backward nearly tripping in my too-tight heels. His eyes narrowed in hatred, and when he spoke his words came straight from his heart.

"Now you listen to me, and you listen good. I didn't talk to you before because it's none of your damn business. I didn't kill Celia Jones and anyone who says I did is a liar. You want to know why I went to that tramp's funeral? Because I wanted to spit on her coffin for what she did to me and my family. I wanted her to know that I had the last laugh. I had the last word on my wife and kid, not her!"

"And you said those words when you shot her through the belly, just like you're saying them now, didn't you!" I shouted out *my* last words, just as two burly brothers dressed like waiters grabbed my arms.

"What the hell are you doing?" I screamed in protest.

"Seeing you to the door, lady," the larger of the two replied.

"Let me go!"

"Sorry, lady. Orders are orders."

"I'll see you in court!" I said, thinking of Jake.

"This is a private club, lady, and you have no business here," the smaller guy said.

"How do you know I'm not a member?"

They looked at each other and laughed, then dragged me through the crowded room and gently tossed me out the front door.

The small crowd that had gathered outside watched without comment as I picked myself up off the sidewalk with as much dignity as I could muster. Head held high, I smiled at the open-mouthed spectators. Thankfully, I didn't have to walk far to my car. I got in without looking at anybody and got the hell out of there as fast as I could.

Although my low-life departure from the high-falutin Businessman's Club hadn't proved much, I'd put Drew Sampson on notice that he might think he was beyond the reach of the law, but he wasn't beyond mine. Besides that, if something happened to me over the next few days, there were a helluva lot of folks who would start paying attention to what I'd said.

I was happy, though, that Larry Walton hadn't been around to see my performance and exit, although I was sure Sampson would tell him about it. I was sorry I'd had to use his name to get into the place, and I hoped they wouldn't penalize him for it. If he ever spoke to me again, I'd apologize.

I headed back to my office to make some notes on my work for the day—namely my conversation with Rebecca Donovan and my impression of Drew Sampson. I also called Detective Griffin and asked if I could drop by his office and talk to him as soon as possible. I hoped he'd let me review his file on Celia, and I wanted to share some of what I knew about Annette and Drew Sampson. Griffin seemed eager to talk to me, which was encouraging. We made an appointment for the following afternoon. I jotted down what I wanted to say to him and then drove home.

It had been a long, grueling day, beginning with my interview with Rebecca Donovan and ending on the sidewalk downtown. My new job was going to start on Monday morning. There were far more big-time impressive detective agencies than Hayle Investigative Services, and I sure didn't want to let Cosey down. I had only a few more days to spend on Celia's and Cecil's murders. With luck, what I told Griffin tomorrow might turn the heat up under the pot, at least enough to get it to simmer.

With the possibility of an increase in funds, I decided to take Jamal to Red Lobster for dinner. We hadn't done that in a while, and it would give me an opportunity to catch up on what he was up to. But when I entered the kitchen, I was greeted by the scent of Calvin Klein for men floating down the stairs followed by my son in his new cashmere sweater.

"Hey, Ma. You home already? I was just on my way to take the bus over to the Clearview to check out that new movie everybody's talking about."

"The bus, huh?" I was his only mode of transportation, so his choice of the bus told me he was meeting a girl and would rather not be seen getting out of his mama's car. "Jamal, it's a school night."

"No, it's not. They're having some kind of teachers' workshop tomorrow, so there's no school."

"How come I didn't know about this?"

"Mom, I gave you the notice! Don't you remember?" He pointed to a xeroxed sheet taped on the refrigerator door. I remembered then that he'd mentioned something about it earlier in the week. I'd been so preoccupied with Celia and her boy, I hadn't half heard him.

"Okay, but I think you should restrict dates to the weekend."

"Date!" He looked alarmed. "Who said anything about a date. I'm just kind of meeting some friends across town for a movie."

"And one of these friends is female?"

He shrugged with a bashful grin.

"So I guess you don't feel like going out to Red Lobster with your tired old mom for some fried shrimp tonight, huh?"

He hesitated, but just for a moment. "No, Mom. Not tonight."

I smiled despite my disappointment. "Be home by midnight. Don't forget your cell, and if you need a ride home, don't be too proud to call me."

"Okay. Love you, Mom," he said, as he headed out the door.

I sat down at my kitchen table, poured myself a glass of chardonnay, then called the Chinese restaurant down the street for some egg foo young and spring rolls, which I polished off in record time. My body was feeling sore from the trip to the sidewalk, so I decided that a warm bath might do me some good. I was just about to climb into the tub when my cell phone rang. I had to dig through my bag to find it. The woman was crying so hard, I didn't recognize her voice.

"Tamara Hayle?"

"Yes, who is this?"

"It's Annette. Annette Sampson. Pik is dead. Drew Junior's best friend Pik is dead. That boy who Drew hung out with. Pik! He's dead! Somebody stabbed him through his heart just like they did Celia's boy. Somebody stabbed him right through the heart."

"What! When did it happen?"

"Pik is dead!" she said again. "My boy is next. Drew is next. Whoever killed Pik is coming after Drew, too. I know it in my heart. I know it in my heart! I'm being punished for Celia. I know the Lord is punishing me for Celia!"

I sat down on the bed, my own heart thumping. "Do the police have any idea who did it?"

"No!"

"Where is your son now?"

"I don't know. I don't know! Please help me!"

"Are you at home?"

"Yes."

"Do you want me to come over there?"

She waited so long before she answered me I thought something had happened to her. But when she finally spoke, her voice was calm. "No, that's okay."

Somebody was with her; I was sure of that. "Are you there alone?"

There was silence, and then a muffled sound, as if she'd put her hand over the receiver. "I can't talk now."

"Are you afraid? Do you want me to call the police?"

"No. Please don't call the police. Definitely don't call the police!"

"Okay. I won't. Are you all right?"

"I'm fine now," she said and did sound better. "Ms. Hayle, are you still there?" she said after a moment.

"Yes, I am."

"What we talked about before, you know when you came to my house, you made me remember something that Celia showed me that might make a difference. I don't think it's important enough to go to the police about, and I couldn't do that even if I wanted to, but I need to talk to you about it. Is that okay?"

"Sure. What is it?"

She hesitated. "I don't want to go into it now. I can't."

"Are you sure you're okay?"

"Yes. I'm fine now. Can we meet tomorrow afternoon?"

"No, I can't tomorrow afternoon," I said, remembering my appointment with Griffin. "How about early tomorrow morning?"

"No, I have another engagement, but Friday afternoon is okay. I'm fine now, really," she added as if she sensed my apprehension.

She did sound better, so we agreed on Friday afternoon at three. But I had a nagging feeling that things weren't right with her, and I couldn't get what she said about the Lord punishing her for Celia out of my mind.

CHAPTER TWELVE

The room was depressing as hell. The walls were a sad blend of institutional gray and brown, and the furnishings a variation on the same tired theme. The air stank of the sweat that comes from hard work, fear, and rage mixed with the smell of overboiled coffee, last night's KFC, and cheap aftershave lotion. In short, this room filled with narrow cubicles and fluorescent lights was like every other squad room I'd ever been in.

I felt a vague sense of discomfort as I gave the young officer at the reception desk my name and waited for him to take me to Detective Griffin. Being in this space brought back both a tragic day in my life along with my memories of the racism and sexism that eventually drove me from the force in Belvington Heights. Those memories were bitter, and I tried hard not to think about them. There was no sense in going to my meeting with Griffin clouded by angry memories of a bunch of evil bastards. Griffin was a good man, I knew that. Most cops I knew were good men, and I couldn't let the memory of a few rotten apples distort my feelings for the whole bunch. Yet I was always uneasy in police precincts; I just couldn't shake it.

Griffin and I spotted each other at the same moment, and his face broke into a grin as the young cop led me to his cubicle. It was one of the largest in the room, which told me he'd achieved some rank since I'd last seen him. Griffin hadn't changed much, although age had taken its toll like it does on everybody. There was just a hint of the reddish-brown hair that once covered his head, and his stocky frame carried more pounds than it should. The deference the younger cop displayed indicated he'd won the respect of those under him, which is no small thing to gain. Citations from half a dozen community groups and photographs of him receiving awards from various city dignitaries decorated the wall behind him as did his diploma from the police academy. He'd been in the class under my brother Johnny, and I recalled how much that fact had comforted me the first time I met him. Always a gentleman, he rose as I entered his cubicle and took my hand.

"Tamara Hayle, it's good to see you again. I'm glad the circumstances are different this time."

"Thank you so much for giving me this time, Detective," I said, settling into the rocky chair across from him.

"How's that son of yours? Jamal, isn't it?"

I eagerly filled him in on what Jamal was doing, and how much I would miss him when he went off to school. Griffin smiled at that, and we both chuckled about how quickly time passes and children grow up. I was touched by his interest in my son and reminded again of how kind he'd been to us on the day that Jamal's half brother was murdered. After a few more moments of niceties, he discreetly glanced at his watch, a subtle indication that it was time to explain why I'd come.

The mention of Celia Jones brought a sad nod that made me wonder if they were any closer to solving her case than he'd been a month ago. Cecil's name, however, brought a different response.

"We're reasonably sure we've identified the person who killed the boy," he said with a self-satisfied smile. "As a matter of fact, we were on the verge of making an arrest when, shall we say, fate stepped in and took charge of the situation."

"Fate? What do you mean?"

"Well, let's leave it at that for now." He was a good cop, and knew better than to compromise an investigation by sharing information that shouldn't be shared. His eyes softened momentarily and he added, "It's a sad thing what's happening in our neighborhoods. Kids with guns. Kids with knives. Well, in my day, well, I won't even go into that, but the kid who murdered young Cecil—"

"Kid? Are you sure it was a kid?" His response surprised and disturbed me.

"We're *very* sure," he said. "As for Celia Jones? There, we're not so sure, but we have a couple of good leads. Could I ask you what your interest is in these cases?"

"Someone hired me to find out who killed Celia Jones."

"So they didn't like the progress we were making, eh?" he said with a self-deprecating chuckle that let me know I was stepping into his territory.

"It was her son."

He looked skeptical. "The kid who was stabbed?"

"Yes, Cecil Jones. He came by my office a few days before he was murdered, and said that he wanted to talk to me about finding his mother's killer. He dropped off some things. A journal she was keeping, a few knickknacks, a—"

I could hear the annoyance in Griffin's voice when he interrupted me. "Journal? What kind of journal? Why didn't you bring these things in? And what were these knickknacks?"

"There was a piece of jewelry that I didn't think had anything to do with the murder, and the journal was the property of her son. I didn't feel I should turn it over to anybody without his permission."

"But he's dead."

"I know."

"It could have been helpful to us. You should have known better," he said, scolding me like an annoyed parent, and I found myself responding like a naughty child.

"Well, I know, I should have, Detective Griffin, but, well, it belonged to the kid. It was his property after all, and I thought he was coming back."

I didn't bother to add what we both knew, that as a private investigator my first responsibility was to my client and not to the police, thus any property that I received from him should go back to him or his heirs, which in this case might be Cristal's baby son. But I also knew that Griffin was doing me a favor by talking to me about an open investigation. There was no need to rub it in his face; I needed to stay on his good side.

But he didn't back down. "You were a good cop, and you're a good private detective, Ms. Hayle. You should have brought the book in. It might have something in it that would be helpful. You know as well as I do that if clues aren't found, if you don't interview witnesses in the first twenty-four hours after a crime, it's harder than hell to solve it. We're lucky—"

"I'm sorry I didn't bring it in, but I've done some research on my own that I think might be helpful," I interrupted him, eager to share what I knew and reinstate myself as a responsible member of the law enforcement establishment.

Griffin moved to the chair beside me, pulling it around to face me so that we were eye to eye. I took it as a good sign; he was ready to listen. "Why don't you tell me what you have, and I'll see what we can do with it," he said, his eyes fixed on mine.

"Well, I mentioned the book," I said, glad to have his attention.

"Which I want to see as soon as possible."

"Yes. Well, she'd written some names in it and telephone numbers."

Griffin picked up a pad and pencil waiting for me to continue. "Annette Sampson, Aaron Dawson, and Rebecca Donovan," I said.

"Clayton Donovan's wife? Shame about the judge, wasn't it?"

"She introduced Celia to Annette Sampson."

If he was surprised by the names I mentioned he didn't show it. But I'd been trained as a cop, too, and I knew never to show what I really felt. That was one of the rules of the interview, and although I was doing the talking, I realized suddenly that I was the one being interviewed.

"So what else was in the book?"

"Well, there were the telephone numbers, some scribbling, letters from the alphabet that made no sense. I called the telephone numbers and I've done some informal interviews."

"With who?"

For the first time, I detected irritation in his voice. "Well, I spoke to Annette Sampson, Rebecca Donovan, and Larry Walton. I also had an unfortunate run-in with the boy's father. Brent Liston. By the way, did Celia Jones have a restraining order against him?"

Alarm registered on his face. "Against Brent Liston? Not that I know of. What did he do to you?"

"He threatened me."

"If he does that again, call us immediately, do you understand? *You* may have to get a restraining order against him."

"Thank you, but I can take care of myself," I said.

He looked at me uneasily and then continued, "So what do you think Larry Walton has to do with this?"

"He knew Celia Jones."

"Walton's the guy who sells cars, right?"

"Yes."

"My wife bought a car from him last year. Sweetheart of a deal. Helluva nice guy. So you said you interviewed him because he knew Celia Jones, right?"

"Yes."

"If the number of men in Newark who *knew* Celia Jones were interviewed, we'd have to talk to half the city," he said with an ironic smile. "Did you say that Walton's name was in her book?"

"No, it wasn't. Actually our interview was informal. I ran into Larry Walton when I bought a car from him, and I remembered him from high school, when Celia and I were best friends."

"Wait a minute. So *you* were close to Celia Jones?"

"Well, I hadn't seen her in a number of years." I knew by the tilt of his head that my objectivity was being questioned. I hoped my answer would dispel his skepticism.

"And you bought a car from Larry Walton, the guy you ended up interviewing?"

"Well, it was a coincidence," I said, uncomfortably aware of the subtle criticism of my professionalism.

"Where did you interview him?"

"Well, as I mentioned, it was quite informal. It took place in a restaurant in Newark. Jay's."

He all but rolled his eyes. "Jay's. I see. So what did you find out?"

"Were you aware that Celia Jones was involved with Drew Sampson's wife, Annette Sampson?"

"Yes." His slow pronunciation of the word told me my information was anything but a revelation.

"And so, I guess, they were both questioned by the police?"

"What else do you know about Celia Jones?" he asked, ignoring my question and reminding me that he, not I, was in charge of this discussion.

"Well, I know that Aaron Dawson was her last boyfriend. I also know that she was pregnant."

"She told you that?"

"No. Like I said, I hadn't seen Celia in a number of years." Was he trying to catch *me* in some kind of a lie?

"Then how do you know she was pregnant?"

"Annette Sampson told me."

"What else did Mrs. Sampson tell you?" His interest seemed to perk up.

"Well, that she was in love with Celia Jones, and that her husband was furious about the relationship. She also stated to me that she suspected that her husband had something to do with Celia's death. That he was capable of murder." I studied Griffin's face for some sign of what was on his mind, but for all the expression he showed we could have been discussing a recipe for barbecue sauce.

"I think that both he as well as the boyfriend, who I have not been able to contact, may have had something to do with Ms. Jones's murder. I think that her son, Cecil Jones, knew or saw something he shouldn't have, some small thing that could identify the killer, and that was why he was murdered, too. I believe that the same person killed them both."

"And this is all from Annette Sampson, Celia Jones's ex-lover."

"No, this is my theory."

"And could I ask, what led you to that conclusion? Woman's intuition?"

His tone wasn't nasty, but rather patient, as if he were responding to some dumb-ass theory tossed out by some dumb-ass rookie. I realized then that I was on the verge of making a fool of myself. For a hot minute, I considered apologizing for wasting his time, using the old standby excuse that I hadn't been sleeping well and was under considerable strain. Then I could rise with some degree of dignity, thank him for his valuable time, and quickly leave his office with my tail between my legs. But that felt cowardly, and truth is, I'd rather be a fool than a coward.

"No, Detective Griffin, it's not woman's intuition," I said firmly, although I knew very well that most of it was. "I haven't been able to get in touch with Aaron Dawson. I was hoping that you'd be able to tell me how to locate him. I also spoke to Drew Sampson, Annette Sampson's husband, and, frankly, I was shocked by the level of his anger and hatred toward Celia Jones. As we both know, violence against women often springs from jealousy, and I think his motive for killing Celia Jones was anger and jealousy about her relationship with his wife, which would be quite a blow to a macho guy like him. I'm also sure that on closer examination, his alibi won't hold up. He has also stated publicly that he will soon be leaving the country, and I suspect his will be a permanent move to a place from which he can't be extradited."

"What about the wife? Annette Sampson? She would have more reason to kill Celia Jones than her husband since she left her husband for Celia Jones and then Jones left her."

"I don't think she did it. She was angry, but she didn't strike me as a killer."

"And the husband did? I don't have to tell you, Ms. Hayle, that killers don't have horns, tails, and pitchforks. They look just like you and me."

"I'm aware of that," I said, feeling like the dumb rookie cop again.

"So then, this is what you *think* you know about the murder of Celia Jones: that she was pregnant. That she was shot in a jealous rage by either her boyfriend Aaron Dawson, who you haven't talked to, or by Drew Sampson, who you admit has an alibi, and that her son Cecil was murdered by the same person because he saw or knew something that would tie the murderer to his mother's death. Is that it?"

"Well, not exactly, I—"

He rose slowly and moved back behind his desk, stepping back into his role as authority and letting me know that my time with him was just about up. He picked up his phone, and asked for a copy of the case file on Celia Jones, which was promptly brought to him. He handed it to me.

I opened it with a feeling of dread. It contained all the paperwork, reports, and newspaper articles about my old friend's death. I read the death certificate and autopsy report and examined the grisly photographs from the crime scene. Even after all these years, seeing Celia's face again, as dead as it was, brought tears to my eyes. I tried to swallow them down. The last thing on earth I wanted was for this man to see me cry, but the tears came anyway. I closed the folder and handed it back to Griffin without looking at him. He opened his drawer and pulled out some tissues, which were soft and scented like lotion, and then spoke to me in a gentle, paternal voice.

"As you can see, Celia Jones was *not* pregnant, the autopsy report states that clearly. She was murdered at approximately eight A.M. with a .22 caliber handgun. Her boyfriend Aaron Dawson, whom we spoke to at length, left her at six A.M. to visit his mother. As you may recall, it was New Year's Day, and he wanted to take his mother to an early service at her church. His alibi for where he was at the time of Ms. Jones's death is not only his mother, and mothers are known to cover for their sons, but the minister of his mother's church and half the congregation.

"Whoever killed Celia Jones waited patiently for him to leave. The person who killed her was a friend or acquaintance because there was no sign of a break-in or a struggle. Neighbors thought the gunshots were firecrackers that someone had set off late to celebrate the holiday, so they didn't report anything. She lived in the kind of neighborhood where they don't report that kind of thing.

"We think the murderer must have been a jealous lover. We're still not sure who, but we're investigating all those with a motive. You're right about the Sampsons, but our focus is on the wife, not the husband. We're just not prepared to move in that direction yet, but we will be shortly. Her husband has a strong alibi. As you probably know, it's Larry Walton. We're not so sure about the wife. Brent Liston, our first suspect, also has an alibi. He was with some woman named Beanie, aka Bernadette Reese."

We sat there silently for a moment or two. "Would you like a glass of water?"

"No, I'm fine," I said, although I was anything but.

"If you don't mind, I'd like to offer you a piece of advice, one good cop to another."

I nodded meekly, a repentant child glad to still be considered one of the fold.

"First, stay the hell away from Brent Liston. He's violent, dangerous, and quick to anger. Second, don't make any public accusations about Drew Sampson. He's a very powerful man with friends in high places. He's also a vindictive, nasty son of a bitch; I know that from personal experience. He wouldn't hesitate to prevail upon his friends to pull your license, and I'd hate to see that happen. Understand?"

I nodded that I did.

"And something else." His voice softened and I could see the kind eyes of the cop who had helped me through that difficult day so many years ago. "You're too involved in this case, Tamara. You know as well as I do that it's never wise for an officer to investigate the murder of someone he or she knew personally because you get too caught up in your emotions and you can't see things clearly.

"If I'm not mistaken, her son was about the same age as Hakim, your son's half brother. That has probably raked up feelings of grief and vulnerability that you thought you'd buried, and it's affecting your judgment. As I said before, we're almost a hundred percent sure who killed the boy and, sooner or later, we're going to find out who killed his mother. Give yourself a break. Go home. Rest. Take care of your kid and thank God he's alive. Let us do our job. That's what you pay us for."

With that he took out his reading glasses and picked up a paper from the pile on his desk, gently indicating that it was time for me to go.

"Girl, I heard about what happened to you over at that Businessman's Club last Wednesday," Wyvetta Green said with a sassy wink as I strolled into Jan's Beauty Biscuit on Friday morning. It was a cold, rainy day and I was looking forward to the comfort of the Biscuit. "I guess those stuck-up fools found out they better not mess with Ms. Tamara Hayle, licensed private investigator. She knows how to turn out a party!"

I cringed as I settled into one of the cerise chairs in the Biscuit's cozy waiting area. Many had been the time this rose-colored room, filled as it was with the smell of herbal shampoo, coconut hair conditioner, and nail polish remover, had been a welcome respite from life's daily woes, but not today. A woman a bit older than me, in jeans and a gray T-shirt with the words "Memorial Hospital" in red lettering, sat next to me. Lucky for me, she was so engrossed in the latest issue of *Essence* magazine she didn't hear Wyvetta's comment.

"Well, Ms. Tamara Hayle, just what you got to say for yourself?" Wyvetta was determined not to let it go. I threw her a nasty look, tempted to get her off the subject by mentioning her hair. She had streaked it an odd color of maroon that picked up the shade of her fingernail polish but contrasted starkly with her turquoise eye shadow. Some days, Wyvetta's "look" was successful; this morning wasn't one of them.

"*Please* don't say anything about my hair. They must have put the wrong color in the bottle," Wyvetta muttered, noticing where my gaze had settled.

"If you don't mention Wednesday, I won't mention your hair," I said, and got a nod of agreement from Wyvetta as she applied conditioner to her client's head. Wyvetta and I are good friends, but we know not to cross each other. Our truce, however, came too late.

"The Businessman's Club? My husband is a member of that club. So what happened on Wednesday?" asked her plump client, shooting a critical sidelong glance at Wyvetta. The woman wore bright red lipstick and a green sweater that fit her ample bosom snugly. Her mink coat was casually tossed across the chair next to her and was weighed down by an overstuffed red Coach bag. Wyvetta threw me a helpless look that said things were out of her control, and I slumped farther down into my chair. Wednesday had been bad enough; Thursday was the last straw.

I'd slunk out of the police station after my meeting with Griffin like a beaten-down hound, too dejected to return to my office. I'd gone home, opened a quart of Cherry Garcia, and watched soaps I hadn't seen in years. Griffin was right, I'd decided. I was taking this whole thing too much to heart. Celia Jones was dead, Cecil Jones was dead, and I should, as the good detective advised me, let the police do their job.

Celia hadn't appeared in my dreams since I'd taken on her case, which was a good sign. And if she showed up again, I was going to tell the girl to *please* haunt somebody else. I'd done all I could for her and her child and now it was time for me to look after my own life. Griffin had assured me the cops were certain they knew who killed her son, although he hadn't exactly shared how "fate" had taken a hand in it. Apparently, he and his detectives knew more about both these cases than I did. My "information" about Celia's pregnancy had been embarrassingly false; you sure can't argue with a medical report. I had no idea why Annette Sampson had told me Celia was pregnant or if Celia had lied to her.

Annette Sampson was the one string left dangling in my involvement with this case that needed to be tied. I'd tried to call her early that morning to cancel our appointment, but she hadn't been home. I'd decided that if I couldn't reach her by three, I'd drop by her house and explain things in person, and that would be that. Her call on Wednesday night still had me worried, so I also wanted to make sure she was okay. And I wanted to ask her why she had lied to me about the pregnancy. Once I spoke to her, I could take the rest of the day off in good faith and prepare myself for my meeting on Monday with my new client.

It still troubled me that the police suspected Annette Sampson had something to do with Celia's death. I was sure they had it wrong, and that the deaths of Celia and her son were connected. But I didn't have any proof except my "woman's intuition," as Griffin put it, and in the world of male cops that didn't count for squat. I knew, though, I had to seriously heed his warning about Drew Sampson. Although Griffin didn't admit it to me, I knew he was a good detective, and he had probably grilled Sampson hard about Celia's death. I'd bet that

Sampson's "friends in high places" had come down on him and his boss. Griffin was a decorated cop, and if Sampson could put pressure like that on him, no telling what he would do to me. Besides that, Larry Walton was his alibi. There was no disputing that, and for all I really knew, they could be telling the truth.

Sometimes you simply have to let things go. The sad truth is the bad guys and girls often do get away with it, particularly if they have money and power, and there's not a damn thing you can do. I couldn't afford to ignore the warning Griffin had given me about Drew Sampson. With Jamal headed to college in a few years and this new assignment on the horizon, the last thing I needed was for my license to be suspended.

In celebration of my newly found freedom and the money that would be coming my way, I'd called Wyvetta Green late last night, and begged her to fit me in for a quick fix-me-up. She called back early this morning and said she had a cancellation, and if I could be at her shop before ten she'd do what she could for me. So Jan's Beauty Biscuit was my first stop this gloomy morning, and all I wanted to do was feel Wyvetta's able hands on my neglected scalp. But I was beginning to wish I'd put beauty on hold for another day.

"Well, is anybody going to tell me what happened at the Businessman's Club?" the woman asked again. I was tempted to say it was none of her business, that in the interest of peace, Wyvetta and I had agreed to let the thing go, but sharp-eyed Wyvetta, spotting my inclination, discreetly shook her head. Wyvetta doesn't alienate good-paying clients, and I suspected this woman, with her head full of conditioner and appointment first thing on a Friday morning, was a regular for "the works." She also had that husband in the Businessman's Club, and that mink coat swung over her chair. There were as many beauty shops in town as there were liquor stores and churches, and she could have her pick of beauticians. I was sure Wyvetta regretted the fact she'd referred to the members of her husband's club as "stuck-up fools" earlier in our conversation, and didn't want to stoke further embers of dissatisfaction.

"Teresa Waterman, this is Tamara Hayle," Wyvetta said, gracefully bowing out of the conversation with an introduction. "And this is Tamara Hayle's tale to tell."

The mention of my name caught the interest of the woman in the gray T-shirt sitting next to me. "So you're Tamara Hayle? I've always wondered who you are. You've got that office right above the Biscuit, don't you?"

I nodded as Wyvetta added, "We been neighbors for as long as I been here, and if you ever need help finding some lost somebody or rescuing some poor soul from disaster, this here is the lady to call. She's one of the best in the business. You can take that firsthand from me, Wyvetta Green, owner of Jan's Beauty Biscuit!" I suspected that Wyvetta was trying to make amends by diverting attention from my "tale" to my profession; it didn't work. Gray T-shirt's curiosity was satisfied, but Teresa Waterman's interest had been piqued. She was like a hungry dog with a day-old stew bone.

"That club! If I've told my husband once, I've told him a thousand times, they should make more of an effort to get some female members or they're going to find themselves on the receiving end of a nasty little sex discrimination lawsuit. Wyvetta, why aren't you a member? Or you, Ms. Hayle? I hope that's why you made a scene. It's about time somebody raised hell about it, and that's one way to get their attention." Her eyes eagerly fastened on my face awaiting my response.

The woman in the gray T-shirt came to my rescue. "Do you have a card, Ms. Hayle? One never knows when one is going to need a good private eye."

"And Tamara Hayle is a *good* PI!" Wyvetta Green added.

"So are they going to make you one of the first female members?" asked Teresa Waterman.

"I very much doubt it." I picked up the *Star-Ledger* and started furiously paging through it.

She looked puzzled. "Well, why not?"

"It wasn't exactly what you think," I muttered.

"Ooh, Lord, I know who you are!" Teresa sat up full in her seat, her small eyes brimming with curiosity and disgust. Wyvetta grabbed a towel and wiped away the conditioner that had dripped down her neck. "You're that woman who broke into the club yesterday afternoon and terrorized poor Mr. Sampson, aren't you?"

"Honey, you better lay back down here so I can finish up this head. I got two clients waiting and two more on the way." Wyvetta tossed me an apologetic glance as she pulled the woman back into her seat and squirted a generous amount of conditioner into her hair.

"Now, Wyvetta. Don't put too much of that on, I don't like the way it smells."

"It's good for your hair, honey," Wyvetta said, with a subtle roll of her eyes.

"Good for you!" the woman who was sitting next to me whispered.

"I think that's just terrible for you to have embarrassed yourself and everybody else by trying to insult Mr. Sampson. My husband told me all about it!" said Teresa.

"Did you terrorize that horrible man for the obvious reasons or has he done something new?" muttered the woman in the gray T-shirt in a low voice. "By the way, my name is Laura Hunter. I'm an emergency room nurse at Memorial."

"But why would you do something like that?" Teresa returned to my "embarrassing" behavior.

Ignoring her, I turned toward Laura Hunter. "What are the obvious reasons?" I asked, reaching into my bag and pulling out the business card she requested.

"Well, there was that business with the drugs."

"What kind of drugs?"

"Not the kind you're thinking of," she said with a chuckle. "Prescription drugs. There was a batch of counterfeit drugs that got on the market, and some of them were traced back to his stores. Nobody could ever get anything on him, and maybe he didn't do anything wrong, but it struck a lot of us as funny, since it was only poor black folks, who are predominantly his customers, who were affected."

"So there was never an investigation?"

"Not much of one. I know of at least one patient, though, a lady fighting breast cancer, who died. Now nobody knows if she died because the drugs weren't what they should have been or if she would have died anyway, but it made a lot of us uncomfortable."

"Both my father and my brother are members of the Businessman's Club *and* physicians over at Memorial, and they *both* say that

Drew Sampson had nothing do with that," Teresa Waterman said, emphatically defending both the integrity of the club and her kin.

"I'm sure you're right," Laura Hunter backed down, turning back to her magazine. But I wasn't about to let her read in peace.

"So what do *you* think about Drew Sampson?" I asked her. "What's your impression of him?"

"I don't really know the gentleman, so I'm not comfortable saying too much about him. There was just that incident with the drugs, but other than that, I can't say anything about him one way or the other," she said, clearly unwilling to challenge Teresa Waterman and the authority of the local medical establishment.

"So you haven't heard anything else?" I dug for dirt. To her credit, Laura wasn't about to hand me a shovel.

"I'm afraid the only thing I should really talk about is my own life or the emergency room where I work," she said with a slight smile. "Ask me about that, and I can tell you anything you want to know. Other than that, I probably shouldn't share what I don't know for a fact."

"I didn't know you were a nurse, Laura," said Wyvetta.

"Really, Wyvetta. Well, I've been over at Memorial for the last ten years."

"Is it anything like that TV show *ER?*"

Laura chuckled and shook her head. "Most of the time it's pretty dull, and we sure don't have any young doctors like Eriq LaSalle or George Clooney."

"If you did, I'd be over there tomorrow!" said Wyvetta.

"TV does have a way of making things seem more interesting

than they are in real life," Laura said, putting down her magazine, obviously ready to talk if we wanted to listen.

"I'll give you that," added Teresa Waterman. "My husband owns a waste management company and everybody thinks he's connected to the mob because of *The Sopranos*. Especially with this being Jersey and everything. How many black men do you know who are connected to the Mob? One of my best girlfriends is Italian, and she's as mad as a bee about the stereotypes on that show. She talks about *The Sopranos* the way my mother used to talk about *Amos and Andy*. It's a shame the lies they spread about ethnic groups on TV."

Finding something we could all agree upon, the four of us nodded in unison.

"Well, sometimes my ER does get close to real life, though," Laura said after a few minutes. "Life in an emergency room can be full of sad ironies, just like on TV. Like last summer. I had a terrible thing happen on my shift."

We all turned to Laura, eager to hear what she had to say.

"A woman came in with her husband, who died right in the same cubicle that she'd been in a couple of months before. That shook me up, I'll tell you that."

"What happened to him?" asked Teresa.

"Walking pneumonia," Laura said.

"Really?" I asked, wondering if she was talking about Rebecca and Clayton Donovan.

"I had an uncle who died of that. You got to watch that shit, it will take you right out if you're not careful," Wyvetta said, shaking her head as if trying to dislodge the memory.

"That was Judge Clayton Donovan, wasn't it?" Teresa said, lifting her head again despite Wyvetta's warning.

"Yes, I think he must have been a judge or something important like that because when he died, cops were all over the place. It was a shame though, I felt so sorry for his wife."

"Rebecca?" I asked, although I knew.

"Yes, that was her name. My niece is named Rebecca. It's such a pretty, old-fashioned name, that's why I remember it. Do you know her?"

"We've met. Nice woman."

"Yes, very nice. Not more than three months before he died, she came in with terrible pelvic pain. It was diagnosed as pelvic inflammatory disease. I don't know what caused it, but sometimes an IUD will cause an infection like that. We saw a lot of women with that disorder when that horrible Dalkon Shield was on the market."

"I remember that thing," said Wyvetta with a shudder. "My girlfriend had that thing up in her, damn near sterilized her."

"Well, it did cause a lot of problems," Laura said. "When you see pelvic infections, they can be caused by improperly inserted IUDs. But other things can cause them, too. However a woman gets it, though, if she doesn't catch it in time, it can seal her fallopian tubes and make her infertile. Lord, I guess all this information about the judge's wife is supposed to be confidential, isn't it!"

"Anything you say within these walls is confidential," Wyvetta reminded us, with a warning look at everybody. "My mother, Jan, may she rest in peace, used to say that a beauty parlor is like a church confessional. Ain't nothing said within these walls gets out. So don't you worry, girl. Everything is held in confidence. So what happened to her?"

Laura paused a moment before she spoke. "The woman was devastated, just devastated because that infection had spread so fast. And one of the nurses told me later that she had lost a child to crib death. Sudden Infant Death Syndrome."

"Now you know that's a shame," said Wyvetta.

We were all silent for a moment, each lost in her thoughts.

"My first baby died like that. I was twenty-one, just married, and I thought my world had come to an end," Teresa said, and for a moment the grief she must have felt that day was written on her face. "But I had my husband with me, and even with all his faults, and he does have some faults, we were able to heal and have three more kids, all grown now. Thank God. You never know what pain a woman carries inside her soul."

That was another thing we could all agree upon and we did, each sharing her varied confidences in the warmth and privacy of Wyvetta's shop.

"So, Tamara, tell me this, exactly what did happen to you at the Businessman's Club last Wednesday?" Teresa asked again, but this time the question was asked with humor and honest curiosity, and we all teased her because she wouldn't let the thing go. But we were friends by then, as close anyway as four women could be on a rainy Friday afternoon in a cozy beauty parlor. So I shared the details of my trip to the sidewalks of Newark by way of two burly brothers, and everyone had a good-natured laugh at my expense.

CHAPTER FOURTEEN

E *ven before I heard the kid scream,* I knew something terrible had happened. They had blocked off the sidewalk leading to Annette Sampson's house with yellow tape, and cops were walking around with that look of woe that comes when they've confronted tragic death. An officer, who looked closer in age to my son than to me, stopped me before I could get to the door.

"What business do you have here?"

"I am a friend of Annette Sampson's, and we have an appointment this afternoon." I went with the present tense, hoping for the best, even though DeeEss sat on the stairs of the porch, shaking as if he were coming apart. His wails of grief stunned us both.

"Jesus Christ!" the cop muttered.

"What happened?"

"I feel sorry for the kid."

"Officer, what happened?" He looked at me as if just remembering I was there.

"Suicide. That's the husband there." He nodded toward the house as Drew Sampson ran down the stairs and sat on the curb next to his son. He put his arm around the boy and held him as if he could will away his pain.

"The husband found the body. Good thing the kid was in the car. The husband called us. Who did you say you were?" he asked, suddenly suspicious. He was obviously a rookie, probably just out of the academy, young enough to be more forthcoming with information than he should be, but tragedy takes precedence over training even with hard-core cops; I knew that from experience. The scowl that was now on his face told me "the Cop" was back in charge.

"Sorry, I didn't say. I'm Tamara Hayle, a private investigator." I rummaged through my bag for a copy of my license. He gave it a quick perusal and handed it back.

"This area is closed," he said, giving me no chance to argue.

Lucky for me, I spotted the burly form of my ex-boss Roscoe L. DeLorca, chief of the Belvington Heights Police Department, heading into the house. "By the way, is Chief DeLorca here yet?" I asked with feigned innocence.

"The Chief?" The glassy gaze of respect that fills a rookie's eyes when his boss's name is mentioned changed the officer's expression from that of tough cop to impressionable kid.

"Yeah, DeLorca and I have worked together in the past," I said, casually linking the Chief's name to mine with an exaggerated nod of self-importance.

"I think he just walked inside."

"*I* think it might be a good idea for you to let me talk to him," I said with just enough threat to make the kid think I had some crime-scene authority.

"What did you say your name was again?" There was newfound respect in his voice.

"Tamara Hayle."

He surveyed the area, which except for me and the Sampsons was empty.

"Okay, Ms. Hayle. Do you mind waiting here for a moment? I'll tell the Chief you're here." He scurried into the house in search of DeLorca, and I turned my attention to Drew Sampson and his son.

Seeing the boy again and the strong resemblance he bore to his mother brought on a pang of sorrow. There is no end to grief when someone you love takes his own life. In a corner of your heart, you believe you could have done something to stop him no matter what people tell you. You try to recall your last words to him, your last gestures. If you're lucky enough to remember them, they haunt you; if you can't, that haunts you, too. DeeEss would never understand why his mother chose to leave him. He would never forgive her for doing it, and he would never forgive himself.

I wondered if Drew Sampson had any idea what his son would go through. Despite his feelings toward his wife, I prayed he would handle his son gently and the memory of his mother with tenderness. But knowing what I knew of Drew Sampson, I wasn't so sure. Even now, I thought I could detect the hint of a smirk on his lips. He had won. He had his son back and everything that threatened him, even the boy's mother, was gone. He could take this child now wherever his money would take him. As far away as was needed to enable them both to try to forget what had happened.

Why had she done it? Why had she given this man the last word?

"Well, Hayle. What brings you to this part of the woods?"

I turned to greet the bearish form of Roscoe A. DeLorca and a smile broke out on my face. My first impulse was to hug him, which was out of the question. His smile told me that the impulse was not mine alone. He grabbed my hand instead and gave it a hearty shake, then gave my shoulder an odd tap, similar to the greetings men bestow on each other at football games.

"I'm fine, Chief."

"And the boy?" It was not an idle question asked out of politeness.

The racism that had struck my son the day I quit the police force had wounded the Chief as well. For months afterward, he would call to check on Jamal, and up until very recently, there was always an envelope of money from "your mom's old boss" underneath our Christmas tree.

"He's fine, Chief. Thanks for asking."

"How's the business going? I got a call from some muckety-muck firm over in Short Hills wants to hire you for a job. You start it yet?"

"Next Monday."

"Good for you." He gave me another shoulder punch, macho-style and heavier than the one before it, and nodded toward the rookie cop. "So the kid here says you had something to say to me about what happened here?" An officer approached with a batch of papers. He signed them then turned back to me.

"I had an appointment with Annette Sampson," I said.

"What time was your appointment?"

"Right about now."

"Well, you won't be keeping it."

"I gathered that."

"I hope she wasn't trying to give *you* some kind of a message." It was a typical DeLorca stab at black humor, and I rolled my eyes as he chuckled at his own sick joke. Cops did that sometimes to lighten the sting of tragedy. Make a joke out of it; don't let it get you down. God knew, I'd done my share of it. Funny thing was, it never worked.

"So why don't you tell me—" He stopped suddenly as he noticed the approach of a young reporter from the local paper. "Come on—" he said, taking my arm and ushering me into the house. "Don't forget, this is a crime scene. Don't touch nothing."

"I was trained by the best," I said, and was rewarded with a grin.

I was overcome by sadness as I entered the small gloomy living room. At some point before she died, Annette had kicked off her shoes by the couch, and they lay where she'd left them. One of her fancy glasses with the remnant of what looked like a Bloody Mary was on the coffee table in front of the couch where we'd sat on Tuesday. An uncapped empty bottle of vodka stood beside it. The beautiful pitcher she'd poured our drinks from stood next to that, and that too showed the traces of tomato juice. Although it had stopped raining, the sun wasn't out yet, and the white walls looked gray and dreary. I noticed that the drawing of Celia was missing. I wondered when she had moved it.

"Where was the body found?" I asked DeLorca.

He nodded toward the bedroom. "Her husband found her. They were estranged, but when she didn't answer the door, he took the kid's key and entered the house. The kid had been staying with him for the last few days, and he came by to pick up his kid's clothes. The kid was in the car, thank God. The coroner is in there now. Was she a friend of yours?"

"She's connected to a case I was working on. How did she die?"

DeLorca nodded toward the liquor bottle on the table. "It's pretty obvious. Suicide." He shot me a concerned glance because he knew about my brother, then added, "Probably accidental. Alcohol and pills. À la Marilyn Monroe and every other sad-ass lady trying to bury her sorrow in booze. Her husband said he filled a prescription for Seconals for her a while ago. She probably got drunk, and when the alcohol wasn't doing the trick, took beaucoup pills. There's a half-empty bottle of reds in the medicine cabinet. So she got drunk, took the pills, lost track of how many she took, went to bed, didn't wake up. Death by alcohol and barbiturates. Common as hell."

"So is that your theory or Drew Sampson's?"

"The husband? Besides the obvious, what does he have to do with any of this?"

"Do you know anything about Drew Sampson?"

"Yeah, he owns Sampson's Drugs, what else?" he asked irritably.

"Well, he did own Sampson's Drugs, but he sold it. Do you know the history of the Sampsons?"

"Like what?" His tone reflected puzzlement and annoyance.

I leaned toward him, speaking confidentially. "Annette Sampson, the victim, left him for Celia Jones, a woman who lived in Newark and who was murdered in January. Drew Sampson hated Celia Jones with a passion. He told me so on several occasions."

"So?"

"So, I'm thinking that maybe—"

"Before you go any further, Hayle, exactly how do *you* fit into this?"

"I was hired by Celia Jones's teenage son to find out who killed his mother. Celia Jones, Annette Sampson's former lover, was killed by multiple gunshot wounds on New Year's Day, and as I said, I've heard some very troubling comments from Drew Sampson regarding both his wife and her late girlfriend, and I'm wondering—"

DeLorca's expression made me stop midsentence. The twist of his lips suggested I'd just entered that territory of crackpot incredibility usually reserved for people who claim they've been abducted by aliens. But for the sake of our shared history, he gave me the benefit of a doubt.

"So, Hayle, you're saying that you think that Drew Sampson, who's sitting out on the front porch there grieving with his teenage son, maybe he had something to do with his alcoholic wife's accidental suicide because he sells sleeping pills in his store and he was mad at her for becoming a lesbian, right?"

"Well, I meant that maybe he'd had something to do with—"

"And furthermore, maybe you're suggesting that perhaps he shot Celia Jones, his wife's lover, too. And I understand from the guys in Newark, and, yes, we do pay attention to unsolved murders in Newark, that said Celia Jones was a hot little number who swung both ways and could have been offed by half a dozen people. Right?"

"No, well, I—"

"And you got all this from her teenage son, I assume." He turned back to sign some papers.

"No, actually, her teenage son is dead," I said painfully.

He smirked, and the young cop who had brought me shifted uncomfortably. "Communicating with the dead these days?"

DeLorca was closer than he knew.

"Her son was stabbed shortly after he hired me."

"Hayle, what's going on? You see people and they turn up dead? Maybe I should take back that recommendation I gave you last week in the interest of public safety." His glance and the sneer on his lips told me that he was only half joking. "Your theories are duly noted. Start your new job next week, go home, and leave this alone," he said, essentially repeating what Griffin had told me yesterday afternoon.

But I wasn't yet ready to leave. "Listen, Chief. Drew Sampson was the first person here at the scene of the crime."

"Accidental suicide."

"He could have tampered with the evidence. Maybe had a drink with her, mixed the pills with the alcohol. Maybe found a way—"

Without answering or acknowledging me, DeLorca turned to sign another batch of papers. Fearing that I might end up on the sidewalks of Belvington Heights, I decided to leave it alone. I wandered out of his view into the hall next to the bedroom where Annette Sampson's body lay. The medical examiner spotted me hovering around the doorway and, assuming that I was still on the force, gave me a respectful nod. Moving as if I was part of the group of technicians milling around the scene, I cautiously went into the bathroom to see what I could see.

The only thing of note was a large bottle of orange blossom bath oil near the tub. But even that pointed to DeLorca's theory of accidental death. Maybe she had taken a warm bath to relax herself, had a couple of drinks, then taken the pills.

"Hey, Chief. Better get in here!" somebody shouted from the bedroom. I stepped back into the shadows behind a photographer as DeLorca pushed past me.

"Oh, shit!" somebody said, and I moved in to get a better view.

Annette Sampson's body had been moved from the bed to a gurney; her yellow silk nightgown trailed on the ground. They had covered her with a sheet, and I was thankful for that. I didn't know the woman well, but I wanted to remember her as I'd last seen her on Tuesday— alive.

Officers and technicians were gathered around her empty bed. Several others, including me and the reporter who had weaseled his way into the house, formed a small group outside the room trying to hear what the big discovery was; we weren't disappointed.

"Well, that docs it. That does it." DeLorca dramatically threw his hands in the air. "Somebody bag this stuff up."

A photographer, who I recognized from my years on the force, came into the room with a Polaroid and began to snap photos. From where I stood, I glimpsed a gun being dropped into an evidence bag.

"I thought it was pills and booze," said the reporter who stood next to me. He had a fresh schoolboy's face, and an overeager manner that suggested this was his first big story. "Hey, Johnson, can you tell me what happened here?" he asked the young cop who seemed to be about the same age. "For the old days," he added, suggesting that they had known each other before.

The officer looked doubtful. "Man, you're not even supposed to be in here." He glanced around self-consciously.

"I'll owe you big-time, and you know I always pay," the reporter added with a wink. "Was it pills and alcohol like they said?"

The rookie cop glanced around again. "Yeah, but they found a gun and some kind of drawing under her pillow, that's all."

"So when was the time of death?"

"I don't know, man!"

"Take a guess."

He hesitated. "I think somebody said yesterday morning. But I don't know."

DeLorca, followed by other officers, came bustling out of the room, and the young cop stood to attention.

"Is Tamara Hayle still here?" DeLorca asked him.

I sank into the wall as I edged my way toward the door. He spotted me anyway.

"Hayle! Get over here for a minute!"

I took a deep breath before I obeyed his order.

"You said something earlier about Annette Sampson being involved with Celia somebody or other, right?"

"Yes. Celia Jones." The tone of his voice worried me.

"Is this Celia Jones?" DeLorca handed me a Polaroid of the drawing that Annette had made of Celia.

"Yes, it is."

"You said she was murdered, right? Shot to death?"

"Yes. On New Year's Day. Somebody killed her with a .22 caliber weapon."

"Looks like Annette Sampson's suicide may not have been accidental after all," he said, his face grim.

"What do you mean?"

His expression said that he wasn't sure if he should share it, but then he went ahead and did it anyway.

"Looks like the case you're working on for your dead client is solved. We just found a .22 under Annette Sampson's pillow along with this drawing you just identified. I'll bet my badge it was the gun that killed Celia Jones.

"Guilt finally got to her. It always does in the end, so she took the easy way out. Some booze, some pills, got the drawing and the gun and put them under her pillow and said her good-byes. Surprised she didn't use the gun that killed Celia Jones on herself. That's usually what they do, but who can understand the mind of a killer?" He shook his head sadly. "So I guess that poor kid's mother was not only a suicide but a murderer, too. Let's call it a day, guys," he said to nobody in particular. "Hayle, I'll give you a call if I need anything further," he added as he headed out the door.

Stunned, and not sure what to say or do, I stood where I was in the middle of the hallway. The fact that I'd been formally acknowledged by the Chief as being indirectly involved in the investigation, bought me some extra time on the scene, and I wandered into the living room as the investigators finished gathering their information. Overcome by a strange mixture of frustration and sorrow, I tried to recall my last conversation with Annette Sampson, trying to remember if there had been any hint at all that she'd murdered Celia Jones. She had spoken just a few words in anger.

Celia was a stupid cunt when it came to men, Annette had said, but that had been in reference to Celia's not using condoms and to the fact that she'd gotten pregnant.

Yet Celia Jones hadn't been pregnant. Why had she lied to Annette. Or had Annette simply lied to me?

Even in our brief conversation, I had detected a certain vulnerability in Annette Sampson, in her sympathy for the losses suffered by her friend Rebecca Donovan, in the love she obviously had for her son. Was I wrong about who she really was?

In that late-night call, she'd said she was afraid for the life of her son, afraid that the Lord was punishing her for Celia. Was that her confession that she'd murdered my friend, and that she was awaiting the Lord's judgment? I'd assumed the emotion I heard in her voice was fear, but perhaps guilt was what I heard, overwhelming guilt. Had she decided to punish herself?

Yet it troubled me that I had sat across from this woman, drinking with her, and not seen beneath her seeming warmth to the coldness that must have been there, that could make her aim a gun and shoot it into Celia's womb.

I shook my head, shaking away my questions, acknowledging to myself that I would never know the answer. The sun was shining almost as brightly now as it had been that afternoon. I glanced again at the chair where she'd sat, recalling our conversation as we drank from her pretty crystal glasses.

And her words came back to me.

I never use them when I'm alone. I only use them when I have company, which is rare these days. When I'm alone, I drink out of a plain old, ugly water glass.

Only one of the fancy ones had been on the coffee table. Could its twin have been broken since Tuesday? Had she changed her drinking ritual for this one last drink?

"Come on, ma'am. Move it," the young cop snapped.

I swayed to the left as if I were going to faint.

"Are you okay?" There was concern in his voice.

"This has been a shock to me, such a shock!" I said in the high-pitched hysterical tone I pull out to alarm chauvinistic men. "I knew these two women, Officer. I knew these two women! They were friends of mine." I swayed again, and he grabbed my arm to steady me. "If I could just have a glass of water, a glass of water, please!" I pulled out Jamal's best "begging" set of eyes. They never worked on me, but they might on the cop.

"I don't know—" He glanced in DeLorca's direction. I swayed dramatically to the right.

"I don't think the kitchen sink is part of the crime scene," I whispered, giving his arm a maternal pat. "You stay here on the scene. I can get it myself."

"Okay, ma'am, but make it quick."

With a slow, unsteady gait, I made my way into the kitchen and turned on the tap. Then, careful not to make a sound, I opened the cupboard where Annette had stored her glasses. The glass I was looking for, the match to the one on the coffee table, wasn't on the high shelf where it belonged but rather on the first shelf, next to the everyday glasses.

Someone had put it back in a hurry. It was a person who didn't know the significance of those glasses and her attachment to them, someone who had that appointment I'd asked for on Thursday morning and knew her well enough to share a drink. It was the person who possessed the gun that killed Celia Jones.

I walked out of the house in a daze. I looked for DeLorca, but he was nowhere to be seen. I walked past Drew Sampson and his son, avoiding Sampson's eyes; I didn't want him to see what was in mine. The winter sun was blinding, and I tripped on a crack as I made my way down the sidewalk. I walked fast, not looking to my left or right. I bumped smack into Larry Walton, who was making his way toward Sampson and his son. He was as shocked to see me as I was him.

CHAPTER FIFTEEN

"We seem to be making a habit of bumping into each other in tragic situations. I don't like it," said Larry Walton. "What are you doing here?"

"What about you?"

"I asked you first."

"I had an appointment with Annette Sampson," I said, even though it was none of his business. "We made it several days ago. The cops are saying she committed suicide. They also say she killed Celia, but I have my doubts about that." I watched him carefully for any sign of what he was thinking, but there were no revealing changes in face, voice, or manner. He just heaved out a sigh accompanied with a nod toward Drew Sampson and his son.

"He called me a couple of hours ago and said there was trouble, but he didn't say what it was. The cops wouldn't let me in. He mentioned something about pills and liquor, which I can't say surprised me. Annette has had a drinking problem for years. But he didn't say anything about Celia. What makes them think Annette had something to do with that?"

"They found a gun under her pillow, and they're sure it was the same one that killed Celia. But I don't think Annette killed herself or Celia, and I'm sure of it now," I added.

"What makes you so sure?"

"I have my reasons."

"What do you think happened?"

"I don't think you want to hear it," I said, nodding toward Sampson, who glanced at me with undisguised contempt. Larry gazed at his friend longer than was necessary, then shook his head. I couldn't read what was in his eyes.

"I think we'd better talk. I could use a drink, how about you?"

"Okay," I said, far more interested in what he had to say than drinking with him.

"Restaurant? Bar? Your place? Mine? You choose."

"Do you know where my office is?"

"I can find it."

"Can you meet me there in half an hour? But I don't have anything stronger than tea."

"That's fine." He glanced at Drew Sampson, then away from him, clearly distressed. "I need an hour, though. I want to take Drew and Drew Junior home. I've got to talk to him."

"Exactly what do you owe him?"

He walked away without answering, like a man with something on his mind.

I didn't wait around to watch Sampson's response. I wanted to get back to my office as quickly as I could to make some notes and put down what was on my my mind while things were still fresh. I wasn't sure what part Larry Walton played in all of this;

I had never been sure. It was time for me to try to sort things out.

Who *was* Larry Walton, I wondered, and what did he *really* know? Why *was* he so loyal to Sampson, whom I was sure had something to do with both women's deaths. Sampson had been the first one on the scene of his wife's supposed suicide. He had a key to her place, and he could have paid her a surprise visit early yesterday morning. Or maybe *he* had that morning appointment with her. If the boy had been staying with him like the cops said, maybe he and Annette had gotten together to talk about their son's welfare.

They had been married once. He had given her the prescription for pills. Maybe they'd had a drink—one for old times' sake. I knew from personal experience that Annette would have been up for that. It would be easy to dissolve sleeping pills in liquor beforehand, to make a lethal potion that would work quickly.

As a pharmacist, Sampson knew exactly what would happen and how long it would take if you mixed barbiturates with liquor. Barbiturates depressed brain activity, and alcohol made the drugs work fast. Within thirty minutes, Annette would become so confused and dizzy she'd have no choice but to go to bed. Her blood pressure would drop to a dangerous level, her heartbeat would slow down, and she would slip quickly into a coma. He could have sat there beside her on the bed until she was unconscious, then slip anything he wanted to under her pillow and leave. Within hours, she would be dead.

A chilling thought came to me, one so disturbing I nearly turned my car into traffic. What if my accusations at the Businessman's Club had scared him enough to make him desperate, to make him want to get rid of any suspicious links to Celia's death. Did Annette remember something that would incriminate him? Was that what she wanted to tell me?

Was I responsible for this woman's death?

But maybe I was wrong. God knew, I'd been wrong before.

Maybe Annette Sampson had killed Celia Jones, then herself. Maybe it happened just like everybody said it did.

But there was still the matter of that fancy, misplaced glass.

If not Sampson, then who?

Chessman.

I could almost hear Celia say it. The only proof I had about his feelings toward Celia was his word.

Once a chess player always a chess player, he had told me over brunch. Just how good a chess player was he?

I parked in the lot across from my office, and popped my head into the Biscuit before I headed upstairs.

Obviously between appointments, Wyvetta sat leisurely reading a magazine. Concern came into her eyes when she saw me. "You okay, girl? You look like hell, but your hair still looks good!" she added, giving herself a pat on the back.

"You know that woman I was rushing out to meet at three? Well, she's dead," I said, which brought a gasp from Wyvetta.

"Dead! Oh Lord! What happened? Somebody did her in, huh?" Expectation mixed with morbid curiosity flashed in her eyes.

"No. They think she killed herself."

"Oh Lord in heaven!" Wyvetta shook her head dramatically and raised one hand into the air as if she were in church. "Honey, maybe you should do yourself a favor, go home, make some dinner, and crawl into bed. My five o'clock canceled on me, so if you need something before you hit the road, I got that bourbon if you want to share a couple of shots," she added.

"Maybe later, I got somebody coming by."

"Who?" Her voice was apprehensive.

"You know Larry Walton, the guy who owns Rayson's Used Cars?"

"Yeah, as a matter of fact I do," Wyvetta said with a grin. "Earl bought a used car from him a couple years ago, and it's still on the road. Now that's one good-looking man!" she added with a wink.

I chuckled despite myself, realizing just how much I needed Wyvetta's sense of humor.

"Ain't like that, girl," I said. "I'm through with all that for a while."

"Okay, Tamara Hayle, if that's what you say," Wyvetta added, rolling her eyes.

"Tonight's your late night, right?"

"Usually is, but I had two cancellations. Can you believe that? I got my last one at six o'clock, which is too early for a Friday night. But stop by before you go home, okay? Maybe we can go get something to eat," she added, still anxious about my well-being.

"Sounds good," I said, heading upstairs.

I turned on my computer, straightened up my office, washed out my extra mug, and dusted off the chair across from my desk, remembering with a stab of sorrow that Cecil Jones had been the last person to occupy it. Had I done right by the kid? I wasn't so sure.

After about an hour, I turned off the computer and pulled out my black-and-white notebook, ready to take down anything of note that

Larry might say. He was a punctual man, and he knocked on my door an hour to the minute. I made a pot of tea, settling on chamomile, which would do my jangling nerves some good, and poured two cups.

"Nice place you've got here," he said as we sipped our tea. "Oh, by the way, I sent in my resignation to the Businessman's Club," he said after a moment.

My expression must have betrayed my feelings, because he quickly said, "Listen, maybe you shouldn't have done what you did, attacking Drew in public like that, but they sure as hell didn't have the right to throw a lady out on the sidewalk."

"Sorry I used your name," I muttered.

He waved his hand in a gesture of dismissal that made me recall the incident of his shirt and my greasy fish sandwich so many years before.

"I didn't like the way they treated you. I'm damn sure not going to belong to an organization that will treat a woman with disrespect. The moment I heard about it, I sent in my resignation, and I called other men I do business with and encouraged them to do the same; several of them have. You can expect a formal apology from the chairman very shortly. If you haven't received it by this time next week, let me know."

"Well, that's nice to hear. Thank you," I said, pleasantly surprised. "But that club is not what you wanted to talk to me about, is it?"

"No," he said, dropping his eyes to the floor, obviously not ready to share his thoughts.

"Why don't you tell me?"

"You've got to understand that what I'm about to say is very hard for me. I don't like betraying my friend. But I think I'd better go with what's right, and this feels right to me." He glanced up, his expression anguished. "I trust you, Tamara. I'm going to take your advice on whatever you say I should do."

"Then you've got to tell me."

"This is hard for me."

"It's about Drew Sampson, isn't it?" I asked, my eyes not leaving his.

"Yeah. I just don't know what to think about what happened this afternoon. Annette, well—" He shook his head.

I gave him a moment. "Do you think he had something to do with his wife's death?"

"I don't know what to think. To tell the truth, he didn't seem as upset about Annette's death as he should have been, and that bothers me. He lived with that woman for years before Celia, she bore him a son, and for that alone he should have shown more feeling, but there was nothing."

"What did he say happened?"

"He told me that the boy came back home, to Annette's house, when he found out that his friend Pik had been stabbed to death. Drew Junior was scared out of his wits, and Annette was scared, too. She called Drew that night, and he came by to take his boy to his place. They agreed it would be safer for him there. That was late on Wednesday."

So her son was the one who came into the room when Annette called me Wednesday night. But had he been the only person there?

"So what happened then?"

"Drew said his son was with him until he found the body Friday, which was when he called the cops. They went to pick up the boy's clothes. You know the rest."

"So was his son with him the whole time? Did he leave him alone at any point?"

"I don't know."

"Do you know what happened to my brother?" I said after a moment, going in another direction.

Concern for me came into his eyes. "Yeah. I heard when it happened, but I didn't know how to reach you or I would have. It was a real tragedy. He was a good brother."

"*My* good brother."

"It happened a long time ago."

"Yeah, and that's why I'm bringing it up now. I'm worried about the Sampson kid. Suicide is a terrible legacy for a child. A lot of studies show that if a parent commits suicide, the child is at high risk, too. She didn't seem depressed when I saw her, and she was a smart woman. I don't think Annette would have put her child at risk like that."

"Liquor can change a mood quickly."

"Yes, that's true," I said, conceding that.

"So you don't think she killed herself like the cops say?" He looked worried, and I found that puzzling.

"I think somebody else did it, and the same person must have killed Celia, too, because they had the gun. It was a .22, the same caliber weapon as the one that killed Celia."

"And you think it would be better for Drew Junior to think that his father killed his mother and her lover? That he's a murderer?" He looked at me in disbelief, and I thought hard about what I was going to say before I answered him.

"I think that he has to know the truth, whatever that is. Once a person knows the truth he can learn to deal with it. Lies are what destroy a child, especially a lie like that."

Larry sat for a while, sipping his tea and gazing out my dirty office window. I didn't rush him. I was pretty sure what he had to say, and the fact that he was here showed me he had decided to level with me. Finally he put the mug down and cleared his throat.

"You know we all came up together, me, Drew, Clayton. I can't think of any other men, not any that I had as much feeling for, that I loved as much as I loved the two of them. I would have done anything for Clay and I'd do anything for Drew if it came to that."

"I remember the three of you as teenagers," I said, wondering when he was going to tell me what I wanted to hear.

"It just about killed me when Clay died as sudden as he did. We'd had a lot of fun together. He was wild as hell."

"So I've heard."

"I didn't mention this before, but Clay was the one who put me back in touch with Celia after all these years. He ran into her through Drew. She had contacted Drew looking for a handout, long before she knew his wife, I might add. He gave it to her because Drew can be a very generous dude. Most folks don't know that about him. When Clay died, all I had left was Drew."

"So you felt you had to lie for him about where he was the morning Celia was murdered," I said, eagerly leaping ahead to the point I was sure he was trying to make.

He gave me an odd glance that I wasn't sure how to interpret.

"Most of what I told you was true," he said. "We did get stinking drunk, and I did fall out on his couch. I was still sick about my wife leaving me and about the general state of my life. Clayton, my other best friend, had died in August and it was New Year's Eve, five months to the day of his death. I had been depressed as hell at the thought of being alone on New Year's Eve, so we decided to spend it together. I left early the next morning."

"How early?"

"Around five, maybe six. I'd promised my daughter I'd take her to dinner on New Year's Day, and I wanted to get an early start so I'd be there on time. I just stretched the truth a little, Tamara. I *was* with my daughter on New Year's Day when Celia was killed."

"No, Larry, Celia was killed around eight o'clock in the morning, so you were on the road when Celia was killed, not with your daughter. Why did you lie to me?"

"Because Drew asked me to say I was with him when she was killed."

"You think he killed her, don't you?" I looked him straight in the eye, but despite what most people believe, looking a liar in the eye won't get you anything but a lie told without blinking.

"I don't want to believe it, but maybe he did."

"I'll tell you what you can believe in, Larry," I said after a moment. He had focused his eyes on my window, looking hard at something I couldn't see. When his gaze met mine, I could see there were tears in his eyes. I wasn't sure who he was crying for—Celia, Drew, or himself.

"You can believe in the truth, Larry. The truth always beats out a lie. It's the only thing you can build on. You told me what you know and now I want you to tell the police, because if you gave Drew Sampson an alibi and he killed Celia Jones, then he probably killed his wife, too. And if you don't come clean about what you know, you are as guilty as he is.

"If he's a killer, you could very well be putting your life in danger, and my life, too, for that matter. You don't know what is truly in somebody's heart. You think you know, but you never do, which is why folks are always surprised when the beast living in somebody's soul rears up and bites them on the ass."

He smiled at that, and I offered him some more tea, which he drank without comment until I broke the silence. "Drew Sampson is taking his kid and heading out of the country, isn't he?"

"That's what he told me when I talked to him earlier."

"When did he say he was going?"

"As soon as he can pack."

"I'm going to call a detective I know on the police force here in town and ask if we can have an appointment to see him. Will you come with me?"

"Tell me when and where and we can go in together."

We shook hands then, and I watched him as he went downstairs, his head bowed down, his foot unsteady. He walked like a man who had wrestled with demons and wasn't sure he'd won.

CHAPTER SIXTEEN

As soon as Larry Walton left, I made my call to Detective Griffin. The officer who answered the phone put me on hold for a long time. I wasn't surprised.

"Ah, Ms. Hayle. What can I do for you this evening?" Griffin said when he finally picked up. I detected that trace of annoyance that creeps into the voice of weary public servants forced to deal with a pain in the butt member of society. I could almost see him glancing at his watch.

"Thanks for taking my call, Detective. I know it's late, and I—"

"Yes, Ms. Hayle, you just caught me. I was on my way out the door. My wife has tickets for a concert at NJPAC, and I'm running late. Could this possibly wait until Monday? As a matter of fact, it's going to have to wait until Monday."

"Please don't hang up, sir." I threw in the "sir" for good measure. "I'm sure you heard about what happened over in Belvington Heights this afternoon."

"Yeah. I got a call from DeLorca over there. He wanted some info on Celia Jones confirmed. He mentioned that you were there on some business. By the way, he thinks very highly of you. Well, I guess that solves your case for you. You can go on back to your—"

"She didn't do it!" I said, more loudly than I meant to.

"I beg your pardon?" It wasn't so much a question as a demand for clarification.

"She didn't do it!"

"Do what, kill herself or kill Celia Jones? Every bit of evidence says she did."

"There were a few irregularities at the scene that I'll be sharing with Chief DeLorca shortly. They point to the fact that Annette Sampson didn't commit suicide. If she didn't kill herself, then she didn't kill Celia Jones."

"So you think somebody else killed her?"

"Yes."

"That .22 had her prints all over it. And that drawing she made of Celia Jones found under her pillow points to her guilt and anger. It was as good as a suicide note."

"Someone else could have given her pills mixed with alcohol, placed her fingers on the gun, and planted the drawing of Celia Jones. We both know that what seems is often what's not."

He sighed or yawned, I wasn't sure which. "Please don't tell me that you think this has something to do with Drew Sampson."

I stood my ground. "Yes, I do, and so does Larry Walton." I was bending Larry's words a bit, but Griffin could draw his own conclusions once they spoke.

"Ms. Hayle. This case is on the verge of being closed, and frankly

I'm happy as hell that it's off my desk. I don't want it opened up again over bullshit."

"This isn't bullshit, believe me. I think you'd better hear what Walton has to say."

He didn't say anything for a moment. I didn't know whether he was looking through his calendar or thinking of another way to put me off. "Okay, Monday morning. And it better be early because I have a full schedule."

I was supposed to report to Cosey in Short Hills at 10:00 A.M. If I got to the station early, and put things in Griffin's hands, I could still make my appointment without any problem. The truth would out; I was sure of that. I just needed to give it this last little nudge.

"Yes, early is good for me, too. Will seven o'clock be too early for you?"

"Seven o'clock in the morning! Make it seven-thirty."

"Thank you. I think you'll find it will be worth your while."

"It better be," he snapped, then added, "By the way, we picked up the guy who killed Pik."

"Pik?" The events of the last twenty-four hours had all but erased Pik and what had happened to him from my mind.

"Yeah. The Sampson kid's friend. The kid who was stabbed on Wednesday. When you were here before, I mentioned that we knew who killed Cecil Jones, right, and that fate had taken care of it. Well, Pik killed Cecil Jones, and fate definitely took care of his thuggish little butt."

"You're saying that Pik killed Celia's boy? I thought they were friends!"

"Apparently not. You never know with kids. Here's the way we figure it went down. They had beef over that young girl, Cristal. Anyway, it seems like she was Pik's girl until she started tipping on him with that other kid, Cecil Jones."

"But wasn't it common knowledge that she was seeing Cecil? She had a child by him."

"No. That baby was Pik's. Ever wonder why he called himself Pik? Weird sense of humor, that kid had. He had babies by a couple of different girls. 'Pik' was some kind of crude reference to his sexual organ. He was also known for 'pickin' people, in other words, stabbing them. And he stabbed that Jones kid right through the heart with his knife, with what he liked to call his pick, as in ice pick. Who the hell knows what motivates these damn kids to do what they do!"

I recalled Cecil's funeral and Cristal's reaction to Brent Liston and Beanie's stares at her baby. There had been hatred in Brent Liston's eyes and fear in Cristal's. Now it made sense.

"So Brent Liston killed Pik," I said, realizing just how fate had taken a hand in things.

"You got it. Brent Liston apparently loved something in the world more than his miserable life, and that something was his son. So he took his revenge on the kid who murdered him. He stabbed Pik right through the heart like Pik had his boy. I guess we're lucky the girl wasn't there or she'd probably be dead, too. Violence begets violence. It never ends, does it?" Griffin sounded weary.

"The other kid, the Sampson boy, was lucky, too. No telling what Liston would have done if he'd found him. But after Pik died, we thought he might have had something to do with it, so we kept an eye on him until we had the evidence we needed. His woman put up a fight when we finally picked him up. We thought we'd have to take her down, too."

"Beanie?"

"Was that her name? I knew it was something that started with a 'B' but that wouldn't have been my first choice," he said, chuckling at his own attempt at a joke. "So that's it, Ms. Hayle. Pik killed Cecil Jones, like we suspected, and Cecil Jones's old man killed Pik. He finally admitted it when we questioned him, so that's that."

"And I guess you'd add that Annette Sampson killed Celia Jones then killed herself, and that ties things up nicely, too, right?"

"That's what the evidence points to."

It didn't tie up for me, though, but I wasn't ready to say it.

"You will talk to Larry Walton and me on Monday, right?"

"Yeah, I said I would, didn't I? For what it's worth. Early Monday morning," he said and hung up.

I called Larry Walton, and left a message on his machine telling him that I'd spoken to the detective and requested that he meet me at the precinct Monday morning. I apologized for it being so early, and said I hoped that he would understand. I turned on my computer, waited for it to boot up, called up "redlocket" and added some final notes about Cecil Jones, Pik, and Brent Liston.

It was Friday night, and Jamal was spending the night with a friend, so I decided to take Wyvetta up on her offer for dinner, but she'd already left. I thought about calling Jake to see if he was up for a drink, but changed my mind. If my suspicions about the nature of Jake's relationship with Ramona Covington were true, then he was probably with her. One run-in with Ramona was enough for one week. Finally, I decided to simply head home, maybe stop at the fish fry place on Central Avenue for some fish and coleslaw.

I grabbed my coat and bag, turned off the lights, set my second-rate burglar alarm, and headed to the rest room on my way out. The building was empty and cold as a tomb, and I shivered as I came out of my office, making a mental note to take up the heating problem with my friend Annie, who owns the place. It was also dark; two of the ceiling lights had burned out. Another matter to take up with Ms. Annie B. Landlady. She'd recently installed a new lock on the ladies' room door, which locked when it was closed, and I was happy she'd done that. With fried porgies on my mind, I came out of the rest room heading toward the stairs.

I saw him as the lavatory door closed behind me. He was kneeling in front of my office door. His hat was pulled down low over his face, and the black coat trailed on the floor behind him like a train. He glanced up and around when the door closed, then went back to fiddling with the lock. He wasn't very good at it. It's a cheap lock and any professional with nimble fingers could have jacked it open in a minute flat. I could have done it in two.

I stopped where I stood, my heart pounding so hard I was afraid he could hear it. He was breaking into my place so he probably had a gun. I was alone in this building. My first impulse was to run back into the rest room, but it was too late for that. I'd have to dig through the junk in my bag to find the key again, and he'd hear me sure as hell. If he saw me standing here, he could rush me, shove me back into the bathroom, then lock the door behind us before I had a chance to get away.

I could make a run for it, down the hallway, down the stairs, but I'd have to pass him on the way out, and the stairway was long and steep. If I ran too fast, I'd risk breaking my neck on the way down. Or he could give me a shove to make sure I went down faster than I should.

I stepped back into the shadows and reached for my cell phone, which was on the top of my junk. I'd put 911 on speed dial, and was sure I could put up a noisy enough struggle for the cops to get here within five or ten minutes. I could fight him off until then. But then came the realization that the damn thing needed to be recharged. I always forget to do it. I cursed my forgetfulness. The man looked up again, as if he sensed my presence, then stopped long enough to glance warily to either side. I stepped deeper into the shadowy corner of the door, thankful for the darkness I'd cursed a moment ago. He started working again. The best I could hope for was that he would manage to open it. When the door opened, it would set the alarm off.

And then I smelled it, the same scent that had been in my house that night I'd come back from Jake's, that heavy fragrance that I couldn't quite place but I knew was from my past. It was Tabu, Celia's perfume, the heady, cheap fragrance she'd worn as a kid. Along with my memory came her father, who had been a mean-spirited drunk, not like my own, who was loving if irresponsible when he "got in his cups," as my grandma used to call it, but a mean son of a bitch, who chased his kids out of his house as soon as they had the means and money to go. I never knew what became of her mother.

He used to tease Celia about that perfume, I remembered that. Made her smell like a backstreet whore, he'd tell her, and Celia would throw back her head and laugh that devil-may-care laugh that said she didn't give a damn what he thought, and that he should go back to hell where he came from. But those hateful words, spoken so often to a daughter who felt no love, had taken their toll. Maybe they were the reason she acted out the role he told her she was destined to play; maybe they were why she'd ended up where she did.

"Celia!" I said her name without thinking about it; that fragrance and the pain of that memory brought her back. And at that moment, he opened the door, setting off my cheap-ass alarm. It was louder than I'd remembered, startling both me and him, but it was the chance I was looking for. Before he could get his bearings, I pounced on his back like a wildcat, shoving him headfirst through the door and onto the floor of my office. He sprawled out, hitting the floor with a thud, and I jammed my cell phone into the back of his head. Startled by the screech of the alarm and what he took for a gun, he tossed his hands up over his head and screamed.

"Please don't shoot me! I don't mean no harm. Please don't shoot me!"

He was the poorest excuse for a thief I'd ever seen in my life.

"Who are you? And why in the hell are you wearing that perfume?" The smell of Celia's Tabu was overpowering.

"I'm Aaron. Aaron Dawson. I just wanted to get something that belonged to me. Something that belonged to Celia. Please. Please. I didn't mean you no harm. I loved Celia. I know you were her friend, and I wouldn't do you no harm. I wear the perfume because it reminds me of her."

He looked up and I saw he was the man who had been at Cecil Jones's funeral, the one I assumed was a teacher.

"Keep your head down!" His face hit the floor again and his glasses slipped off his nose, which began to bleed.

"Don't shoot me!"

"Keep your face on the floor. Nose first! Keep your hands overhead, straight. The police are on their way," I said in my tough-girl voice, although I knew the security company hadn't made their call yet to verify that there was a break-in.

"Please, please, please don't let them take me," he pleaded. "It would break my mother's heart if I got arrested for something like this. It would kill her! Please don't let them take me."

Lying on the floor with his face mashed against it, blood dripping from his nose, he looked pathetic. I shook my head in disgust, more sorry for him than angry.

"What the hell are you doing here?"

"Trying to get what belonged to Celia. I didn't mean no harm. I thought you'd left."

"So you've been watching my office?"

"Yes. I'm sorry."

"And you broke into my house?"

"I'm sorry. I'm so sorry. I just wanted to get it. It was all I had left from her!" Blood from his nose dripped onto the floor when he lifted his head.

"Put your damn head down! I should shoot you with this gun right now for breaking into my place and scaring the shit out of me, you stupid son of a bitch." I had a sudden, strong impulse to give him a couple of swift kicks in the butt, but I was taught never to kick a man when he's down, and lessons like that stay with you, so I held myself back. I sure felt like it, though.

"Please don't shoot. Please. There's been enough killing already. Celia and the boy. Please! I just wanted to get it back. It was all I had left. I gave it to her and I just wanted to get it back," he cried out.

"Get what back?"

"My ring. The ring I gave her. My diamond ring! It belonged to my daddy, and I gave it to Celia. I wanted to get it back."

"What made you think I had it?"

"Because Cecil told me he was coming to see you. He told me you were Celia's friend. He said she was trying to contact you before she died. I knew he had come to see you before he died, and I thought maybe he had left it here with you. Because it belonged to his mama and he'd want it to stay safe."

The telephone rang. It was the security company, finally responding to the alarm, about damn time.

"Close your eyes! Keep your hands above your head, your face on the floor. Or I'll shoot you right now!"

"Please, please don't let them take me. Please." I felt a nearly uncontrollable urge to laugh. I stepped over his prone body to the phone and gave the security company my code, then watched Aaron Dawson sweat for another five minutes or so.

"So what can you tell me about Celia Jones if I let you go?"

"Anything," he said, his voice cracking as if he were about to cry. "I'll tell you anything you want to know because I loved that woman more than my own life."

CHAPTER SEVENTEEN

S*o for the third time in less* than two weeks, I sat across from one of Celia's old lovers bent upon telling me a tale of woe. We were in a crappy luncheonette about a block and a half from my office. I've put in enough time with mean-ass Negroes to know this fool was nobody's threat, but there's always that chance that somebody will flip out and turn ugly when you think you've got them pegged. A mistake like that can cost a woman her life. With that in mind, I brought him to this café, which was warm, empty, and reasonably clean. I ordered a cup of coffee and a piece of apple pie. Dawson ordered an orange soda. His hands shook when he dropped in the straw. It did my heart good to know I could still throw a scare into somebody.

It looked like he was dressed in the same clothes he'd worn to the funeral, but he seemed to be the kind of man who would wear the same color and style day in, day out for twenty years and never get tired of it. If I saw him on the street, I never would have pegged him as one of Celia's men. He looked like a mama's boy, if ever there was one, and younger than Celia by about ten years. Maybe that was what she saw in him.

"Thank you for not giving me to the cops," he said after we'd sat down. "I don't know what my mother would have done if she'd had to come and bail me out of jail. Listen, I'm sorry about the break-in, about trying to get into your house, I'm sorry—"

"Don't ever do it again!"

"I was desperate."

"Desperate will get your ass in jail for life. How did you know where I lived?"

"Celia showed me when we first started going out together. I had my mother's car and we were driving somewhere, and Celia said, turn down this street, then she said, my used-to-be-best-friend lives here."

Used-to-be-best-friend. That sounded like her.

"And after all this time you remembered it?"

"It wasn't all that long ago, and anyway, I remember everything she ever told me about herself. And when Cecil told me she was planning to go to see you before she died, I remembered that, too, and that was why I thought you might have that ring."

"Like I told you, the cops have the ring," I said, eager to get him off the damn ring. "Cecil was wearing it when he died, and his father must have gotten it from the funeral director. He had it on his finger the day the boy was buried."

He visibly shuddered, so I added, "I know the cop who is working the case. I'll see if maybe I can help you get it back." Truth was, that ring belonged to Brent Liston because it belonged to his son, and there was no way he was going to get it back, I was certain of that.

But that brought a look of relief from him, and he nodded without saying anything, glancing around the luncheonette as if uneasy. Then he shook his head as if troubling thoughts had entered.

"I never thought when I met her it would end up like this."

"When did you meet her?"

"Last September."

"How?"

"Night school. I teach a course in computer programming in the adult school they run at night at the high school. Celia liked playing around with computers, and she was trying to get into another line of work. She was always trying to improve herself."

I smiled to myself. A love of computers was yet another side of Celia Jones I wouldn't have guessed she had.

"What did she want to become?"

"She thought maybe she wanted to be like an executive assistant, you know, somebody who works in a big office. She liked the idea of working around people who dressed nice, people who went out to lunch and did things like that. She wanted to make things better for herself and her son. But there was always something standing in the way, always somebody or something wouldn't leave her alone."

"Like who? Drew Sampson?" I volunteered the name.

He didn't say anything for a moment. "That's Annette's husband, isn't it?"

"So you know Annette Sampson?" I used the present tense; it was too early in our conversation to let him know she was dead.

"Yeah," he looked down, focusing on his soda. "She thought she was the only one who could do Celia any good. I don't think she likes me very much."

"Who else wouldn't leave her alone?"

He thought for a moment, then added, "Somebody was writing her dirty letters. She showed me a couple, and they were so hateful and mean, so disgusting. I couldn't believe that somebody would say those things about her, would write that kind of filth to her. Celia said she didn't know how somebody could hate her so much for nothing."

"She showed them to you?"

"Yeah."

"What did they say?"

He closed his eyes like a kid does when something scares him.

"I don't like to say those kinds of words," he said, his mouth pursed like a prissy little girl, which brought to mind Old Man Morgan.

"Tell me what the goddamn things said!" I was losing patience.

"You fucking immoral, diseased cunt. You fucking immoral cunt. You fucking immoral diseased cunt. You have no right to live when others have died. That and other things written again and again and again down the page. Other things too nasty to repeat out loud."

"I get the idea. Cecil never mentioned letters to me," I said, as much to myself as to him, but no mother in her right mind would share garbage like that with her son. "Did he know about them?"

"Yeah, I think she may have mentioned them to him, but she didn't want him to be scared for her. She didn't show them to him because they were too mean."

I thought of my own son then, and how I keep things that scare me from him, and my heart softened again toward my old friend and the boy she loved.

"What did they look like? What kind of paper?"

"Nice paper. Like the kind you write invitations on. When she got the first one, Celia thought somebody was inviting her some- where fancy. They had a nice feel to them, that paper. Like silk, al- most. So many nasty words on such pretty paper."

He shook his head with a sad smile, then a light came into his eyes as if he remembered something. "They were written in red, and sometimes the letters were blurred. Not like a pencil or ballpoint pen, but real ink like my daddy used to sign checks before he died. The kind you put into a pen. The writing is prettier when it comes out than it is from a ballpoint pen."

Cunt. That was Annette Sampson's word for Celia. She probably had fountain pens, too, and colored inks.

"Once she said that she thought the letters had something to do with a relationship that came out her past."

"What did she mean by that?"

He shook his head at a loss. "I don't know but I think she meant something that happened a long time ago, that wasn't important to her anymore."

My thoughts swung back to Drew Sampson. Maybe he didn't know that Annette's relationship with Celia was over. Larry said she had asked him for money, and he had generously given it to her. Had there been more to his relationship to Celia Jones than anybody knew?

Dawson began to play with his straw like a kid does when he doesn't know what to do with his hands. "She was going to bring the letters over to you, so you could see them, maybe help her figure out what to do about them, when she got them back from Annette."

"Annette had them?"

"Yeah."

"Did you mention the letters to the police when they questioned you?"

"I told them, but they didn't think it amounted to much. They didn't think it was all that important. I think they misjudged her. I think they thought she was the kind of woman who would get letters like that."

I took a sip of my coffee, and he finished his orange soda, sucking it up loudly.

"You knew the people in her life. Do you have any idea who could have sent them?"

The expression on his face was impossible to read. "I thought it was Annette at first. She felt like Celia had betrayed her because she was mad and jealous when Celia moved out. She said a lot of hateful things to Celia, things you shouldn't say to anybody. I thought it was Annette, and I think Celia thought it might be, too. That was why she took them to her, to confront her, but when she came home she said it wasn't Annette."

"And she was sure it wasn't?"

"She said Annette wanted to keep the letters because she thought she might know who wrote them, but she never told Celia who did."

I wondered why Annette hadn't mentioned them when we spoke. Unless she had confronted the person and thought things were resolved.

"Annette was so mad at her when she broke off with her. She called her all kinds of things," he said as if speaking to himself.

"Annette told me Celia was pregnant with your child, but that wasn't true, was it?"

"Celia told Annette that was why she was leaving her, but she was lying about that. I told Celia to go on and tell the woman the truth, but Celia didn't want to hurt her more than she had to, and figured that lying about why she was leaving, saying she was going to have a baby would make her feel better.

"Celia had herself fixed a couple of years ago. She couldn't have no kids. She said it was hard enough for her to take care of one child without having another. She said she liked to do it without rubbers, and if she was fixed she didn't have to use them."

That piece of information was delivered with a smile that gave me the creeps. Risk-taking had obviously still been part of Celia's behavior. If that gun hadn't killed her, risky sex might have done the job sooner or later. What truly amazed me was the number of lovers—both men and women—who had gone along for the ride. I wondered if Celia had been tested for AIDS and if she could have tested positive. That would have given somebody a reason to shoot her through the womb.

"So you never used condoms when you slept with Celia?"

"No," he said as if puzzled.

"And, considering her history, you weren't afraid of catching AIDS or something?"

"How could you say that about Celia, that she would have something terrible like that! I would have been proud for her to be the mother of my children, if she could have them. I would never have insulted her by suggesting that she could have something like that." His voice was filled with outrage and disdain at my suggestion.

Now this *is* a fool, I said to myself.

"I think you should know something. I found out this afternoon that Annette Sampson is dead. The cops say that she killed herself, and that she killed Celia."

He put his hands over his face, shaking his head from side to side as if absorbing in small doses what I'd just told him.

"No," he said. "I don't believe that. Annette didn't kill Celia. She loved Celia, why would she kill her?"

"I don't know, but that's what the police are saying."

He dropped his hands from his face. "They're wrong." He stared at his soda, playing with the straw and finally pushing it away. "Celia and I spent New Year's Eve together. I left her early in the morning, and then somebody killed her, but it wasn't Annette."

"Do you have any idea who did?"

"No."

"Was she expecting anybody after you left?"

"She just said she hoped this year would be better than last year, and she would see me later on. That's all she said, and the next thing I knew she was dead."

He shook his head in a sad, weary motion. "Cecil said you were the last chance."

"Last chance?"

"The last chance to find out who killed his mother. Celia told him about you, too. The same way she told me, that you were her used-to-be-best-friend. It was just you and him that was left over from her life. You two were the only ones she ever mentioned to me."

I was puzzled. "Me and him, meaning me and Cecil?"

"No. *Him.* That man." He looked at me strangely, as if I should know who he was talking about. "She never told me his name. It was the man she lost her cherry to when she was in high school. The man who she said treated her like nothing and then tried to make up for it when he saw her again. She always said she was a little bit in love with him, but not much because she was in love with me," he added proudly, as if trying to prove something to himself.

"And she never told you who this man was?"

"She said he was an important man now. Big-time. Someone who knew a lot of people and had a lot of influence. She used to say he had respect. Big respect. And that if he could have, he would have helped her again."

"What did she mean by that?" I asked him, but he shrugged, and I wasn't sure if that was all she said or if he was simply tired of talking about it. He looked tired and scared. I wasn't sure why.

"And you don't think this man could have had something to do with Celia's death?"

"She only mentioned him once. We were talking about our past, and I asked her who she had done it with the first time in high school. She was fourteen and he was seventeen. She said she'd been seeing him for a while, but it was over now for good, and that was all she said." He paused for a moment as if still trying to figure out what all this meant, and then added something I knew.

"If Celia didn't want to talk about something she didn't talk about it. When the letters started coming, she said the letters might have something to do with him, and then that was that. She went to Annette with them, then she was going to go to you, and then she was dead. Can I go now?" he asked, as if he were in school or still lying on my floor with my cell phone up against his head.

When I told him he could, he beat it out of that dirty little café like his tail was on fire. I ordered another cup of lousy coffee and thought about what he'd just said.

Him.

Who had she had the biggest crush on? It had been one of the three of them, that much I knew. Larry Walton. Drew Sampson. Clayton Donovan. They had run the school and maybe one of them—or all—had slept with her. But only one had been her "first time," as Dawson put it. What did that past have to do with this present?

A B C D

A for Annette or Aaron. B for Brent. C for Chessman. D for Drew. *Once a chess player always a chess player.*

But hadn't he agreed to go with me to the cops on Monday? Or was that part of his plan, too? Celia Jones had been the only person who knew the truth about their relationship. But maybe there had been another. Maybe Annette Sampson knew something, too. The thing that she had planned to tell me before she was murdered.

Drew Sampson hated Celia Jones, there was no doubt about that. But could their past have been intertwined in ways that nobody knew? Could his feelings have run deeper than anybody guessed? Could he and Chessman be in it together?

A B C D

Or did those letters mean nothing at all?

Annette might have had an alibi for that morning. Rebecca Donovan might have seen or spoken to her then or the night before, and knew more than she should have. One thing I was sure of, she didn't know that Annette Sampson was dead, and that would give someone an advantage. Someone she might trust. Someone who knew where to find her. The hair stood up on my neck then, like it does when a breeze hits it wrong or somebody evil walks across my grave. Rebecca Donovan was in danger, I was sure of that now. I had to let her know it before she became his victim, too.

CHAPTER EIGHTEEN

I *went back to my office* and called Rebecca Donovan. Her answering service told me she was out of town, which I already knew. I told the woman who answered the phone that it was a matter of "life and death," and she promised to relay my message "when Ms. Donovan called," but I was sure it wouldn't be relayed with the proper urgency.

My only chance of warning her was to tell her in person, which meant I'd have to find out wherever the hell she was in Connecticut and either convince her to come home or ask her to alert the proper authorities. I couldn't remember the name of the town, although I was certain that it started with an "A," so I tried to access a map of Connecticut on the Net, but the dial-up service on my old-ass computer took so long, I decided to use Jamal's computer at home. Friday night was a late night for my fish fry place, so I picked up a sandwich, fries, and a tossed salad to make me feel virtuous and headed home. After I'd eaten, I went through Jamal's geography software and scrolled through Connecticut cities and towns, until I found one that sounded familiar: Ashton, Connecticut. Population 2,100, founded in 1710.

The town was in the eastern part of the state, about a three-hour drive from Jersey. I'd be lying if I said I didn't feel like forgetting the whole thing, and spending my Saturday morning doing nothing, like I usually do, but if something happened to the woman, it would be with me for the rest of my life. Besides that, I'd get a chance to test out my new car on a serious road trip. If I left by seven, I'd be there around ten, a decent enough hour to drop in on somebody with bad news. I would offer a shoulder to cry on along with any assistance I could, treat myself to lunch at a country restaurant somewhere, and be back home in time to take Jamal to Red Lobster. I got directions from MapQuest (Jamal would be proud of me!), took a warm bath, and was in bed by eleven. Sleep didn't come easily, though. I woke up at four in the morning with a dozen what-ifs racing through my mind.

What if Annette had told Rebecca what she was planning to tell me before she was murdered and her killer knew it? *What if* he was trying to get to her before she found out about Annette? *What if* he had killed her already? *What if* he was still there? That last what-if made me jump up in the middle of the night and drop my .38 into my Kenya bag.

Drew Sampson was on my mind when I unlocked the safe where I keep it, and Larry Walton wasn't far behind, although I didn't want to believe it was him. He had always seemed like a nice man, but anyone can change from good to bad to worse. I wished now I'd gone ahead and called his ex-wife again to verify where he was when Celia was killed. Maybe he had gambled on my not doing it. His business depended on knowing what people would and wouldn't do. Maybe he had given me the number assuming I wouldn't call.

At this point, I didn't know *what* the truth was about anybody— not Drew Sampson or Larry Walton. What I *did* know, though, was that a cell phone up against the back of the head wouldn't fool either of them. I don't like guns, but I needed to be able to protect myself and anybody else who needed protection.

Later that morning, I put a slice of leftover fish into the micro- wave, made some strong coffee, and hit the Parkway with Cassandra Wilson and Mary J blasting from my CD player. It started snowing around eight-thirty. It was a slushy mess, melting before my wipers could hit it good, but it was sticking to the road. There was no traffic; anybody with good sense was still in bed, and I drove cautiously, fear- ful of sliding. Jamal would never forgive me if I wrecked our new car.

Snow was coming down hard by the time I got to Hartford, and the roads were dangerously slippery. I don't have much experience driving in the snow. In the city, it turns to mush the moment it hits the ground. It was Saturday, so the snowplows were taking their sweet time getting out. If the roads got worse, I'd probably have to check into a motel. More than likely, though, Rebecca Donovan would offer to put me up for the night, and that meant I'd have to call Jake and ask him to let Jamal stay with him. I hadn't spoken to Jake since my last visit. Maybe it was pride or just old-fashioned stubborn- ness, but I was determined to wait for him to call me.

I thought about him as I drove. The snow falling softly on my windshield and Cassandra's sensual, mellow voice reminded me of the tenderness I've always felt for the man. With or without Ramona

Covington, there would always be a place for him in my heart. The question was, how big a place would it be and would anybody else ever fill it?

Jake was on my mind as I passed the sign for Ashton and pulled into a 7-Eleven for gas. In Connecticut, as in most other states beside Jersey, you can pump your own gas, so after I'd filled my tank I went into the store to pay and check the phone book for Donovan; I hoped they were listed. There was a C. Donovan on Ebbets Road, and I assumed that was her. I called the number, but nobody answered. I hoped Rebecca hadn't changed her mind and gone somewhere else. Or that somebody hadn't reached her before me. I didn't want to think about that.

"Getting bad out," the man behind the counter said when I paid for the gas. He had a chiseled, thin face with the hint of a beard and an elfish grin. He looked too old to be working at a convenience store in weather like this. I made a mental note to check the status of my SEP/IRA.

"Yeah, it's coming down."

"You new to these parts?"

"Actually, I'm looking for a friend."

"Donovans?"

I had to smile and was tempted to say "no" just to throw him off. "Yes, do they live far from here?"

"Ebbets Road. Right down the road. Judge Donovan used to come in here all the time to pick up the *New York Times* when he was with us. Not too many folks here take the *New York Times* every morning, but he was in here like clockwork, every day at eight A.M. to pick up his paper. She, the missus, came in here this morning to pick up some rock salt, though. Nice lady, Mrs. Donovan. Shame what happened."

"Yes it was," I said, thankful that she was home, but wondering why she hadn't answered the phone. At least she was alive this morning.

"Nice people," he added again.

"So, has anybody else stopped by to get gas, somebody who might be looking for them?" I asked.

"Somebody from out of town looking for Mrs. Donovan?" His tone said that "out of town" was a euphemism for "black person." "Not on a day like this."

"How do I get to Ebbets Road?" I asked as I slipped the change from my twenty into my bag.

"She didn't tell you?" His eyes were suddenly suspicious. "The roads around here are tricky. Most folks give their guests directions."

"She did, but would you believe I left them on the kitchen table, along with her number!" I squeaked out a silly-little-me giggle.

"Not hard. Stay on this road about six miles. Take a left on Rankin Road, then turn right on Ebbets. Name's on the box. It's green, I think."

I thanked him, went back to my car, and cautiously pulled onto the road. A snowplow trudged ahead of me, and I was grateful for that. It was snowing so hard, I could barely see the road.

What if he was still there?

I took the left onto Rankin Road and then on to Ebbets Road with a sense of foreboding.

It was a beautiful country road, and under different circumstances, I would have enjoyed the view. The road was narrow and curvy, and the trees hanging over the road were heavy with snow, and looked as if they belonged on a Christmas card. The houses were set back from the road, but I easily spotted the Donovan's bright green mailbox and pulled to the curb. It was a small, white house with green shutters that matched the mailbox. Snow had piled up high in the driveway, and several lights were burning in the living room; smoke drifted from the chimney.

But there was still a chance that somebody was with her, a surprise visitor sitting on the couch, sipping the fresh coffee she'd made, finding out what she knew before he did what he'd come to do. A black Mercedes-Benz with Jersey plates was parked in the driveway. It could be hers, but if she'd had enough foresight to buy rock salt, she would have had enough to park her car in the garage. I placed my gun near the top of my bag, strewing some stray Kleenex over it so I could get to it quickly, then trudged up the snowy driveway.

The porch was small, but large enough for an old-fashioned swing, which made eerie squeaks as it swung in the cold wind. The curtains in the window nearest the door were open, and I glanced inside. A fire blazing in the fireplace radiated a warm coziness. But the room was empty, and I felt that intuitive sense of dread, which has warned me of danger more times than I care to remember. I thought again about leaving while I could, maybe contacting the local police department. But recent run-ins with city departments had left me wary of sharing my theories until I had hard evidence to back them up.

But then Rebecca came into the room, and gave the fire a poke. She settled into a large comfortable-looking rocking chair, which looked like it might have been the favored chair of her late husband.

She was dressed in an elegant black robe that clung to her body like silk, and seemed strangely incongruous with the setting. I watched her for a moment then pressed the doorbell. Startled, she glanced toward the porch, and I waved from the window.

"Mrs. Donovan, I'm sorry to bother you, I hope I didn't startle you," I said when she opened the door. She stared at me blankly, not speaking.

"I'm Tamara Hayle," I said quickly, fearing she didn't recognize me. "We spoke several days ago?"

"Why are you here?" There was no expression in her eyes.

"I'm afraid I have some very sad news. I tried to call you, but your answering service wouldn't give me your number, you don't have an answering machine, and I felt it was very, very important that you know."

Truth was, I was beginning to wonder how important it really was. Had I made a mistake?

"Come in," she said as if it had suddenly occurred to her that I was standing outside in the snow. She took my coat and hung it in the closet. I set my Kenya bag on the coffee table in front of the couch and moved closer to warm myself by the fire. Her manner surprised me.

The blazing fire, chintz curtains, and matching upholstery gave the place an ambience of homey comfort. There was a stairway on the side of the room that led to what I assumed were the upstairs bedrooms, and a door that was ajar probably led to a kitchen. Yet there was something unsettling about the room. For one thing, the photographs that had been in the Newark house were here as well. I wondered if she kept duplicates, one for each home. There was one thing, however, that was clearly not a duplicate. The black porcelain urn with the golden lid that I had admired before sat on a pedestal close to the rocking chair.

So she carried it around with her, this urn with her husband's ashes. Did she set it beside her bed at night? Or across from her in the dining room or kitchen?

"What brings you here, Ms. Hayle?" The cold distance that had been in her voice before was back.

But what did I expect, showing up on this woman's doorstep in the middle of a snowstorm. I was probably lucky she let me in at all. I got right to the point.

"Something terrible has happened, that I thought you should know about, and I wanted to tell you as soon as I could. First of all, is there anyone else here?"

She paused a moment. "No." She glanced at the urn, and I wondered if that was the presence that had put the hesitation into her voice.

"I saw the black car—"

"That's my car. It's a one-car garage. I park Clayton's Porsche in the garage."

Did she put his ashes in his car and drive around? Talk to him as "he" rode beside her?

"Oh, I see," I said. "Well, I have some very sad news for you. You may want to sit down," I started slow, took a deep breath. "I thought you should know as soon as possible that your friend, Annette Sampson, has passed away. Actually, I had an appointment to see her on Friday, and when I visited her home the police were there. They think that her death occurred sometime Thursday, but her body was found by her husband on Friday morning. I'm so sorry to be the one to have to tell you this. Actually, I was—"

I stopped midsentence because there was no reaction from her, nothing at all. Could this be a form of grief? I wondered.

"And you came all this way in this weather, all the way up here just to tell me that? Or is there something else?"

I thought then about Aaron Dawson's reaction, the hands over his face, the way his body shook.

"Yes. I thought you should know."

"What was your appointment with her about?" There was warmth in her voice, but there was also cunning as if she wanted to pry something from me that I didn't want to tell.

"A personal matter."

She glanced at the urn, and then, as if she realized how odd her reaction had been, she tried again, covering her face with her hands as if weeping. "Oh, poor Annette. I'm so sorry to hear that!"

Perhaps I was judging her too harshly. Maybe it had taken that long for it to get to her, for her to understand my words.

"Yes. I was sorry, too."

We sat there in silence, the gaze of both of us drawn to the crackling fire. I risked a glance at her. "You don't get lonely here?"

"I like it here by myself. People take me from my thoughts."

And your memories, I thought. I could see through the window that the snow was falling harder. A sheet of white covered the picture window in the dining room. It was painfully clear that any hope I had of her offering me shelter from the storm was out of the question. Best for me to get on the road as soon as I could. I stole another glance at Rebecca, still puzzled by her response to Annette's death and the odd mood that had overtaken her.

"The authorities assume that Annette killed herself because she killed Celia Jones," I said, hoping to get some kind of a rise out of her, anything besides the silence, and I got one: a smile that was barely perceptible, but her eyes were still glued to the fire.

"Could I trouble you for some coffee or tea? It's a long drive back to Jersey, and I want to get on the road before it gets too much later," I asked. She glanced from the fire at me.

"Yes, that's a good idea. I'll make some for you, right away."

"On second thought, don't bother." That feeling of dread was back.

"It's no bother."

"Thank you," I said, grateful for a few more moments before the fire, but something wasn't right about this woman, and I wanted to be out of there as soon as possible. Now more than ever, I felt that I'd been on a fool's errand. I'd wasted my Saturday, put more mileage on my car than I needed to, risked my life in this damn storm, because I was worried about her safety, and she was treating me like crap. This would be one to share with Wyvetta and her customers in the Biscuit.

Always the lady, Rebecca brought in the coffee in a carafe with a mug and some cream and placed it on the coffee table.

"Thank you so much," I said, reaching for the carafe, not waiting for her to bother to pour it. In my haste, I knocked it over, spilling coffee over the table. A photograph of her husband was in harm's way, and she screamed as she grabbed it, knocking my Kenya bag out of the way; the gun inside it made a thud as it hit the floor. She examined the photograph in her hand. Coffee had seeped inside. When she looked up at me, I was surprised by the rage in her eyes.

"I'm so sorry," I stuttered, as I swooped another picture off the table before the coffee could reach that one, too.

"It's ruined now, and there will never be another one taken. Never."

"I'm really sorry," I stammered again. She seemed stunned, unable to move. "Let me get something to wipe up this mess," I said as I grabbed the tray and coffee and fled to the kitchen in search of paper towels. I'd get myself some coffee on the road, I decided. Maybe stop at that 7-Eleven on the way back to the highway. The counter guy would be better company.

With a nasty attitude, I poured the coffee out of the carafe, rinsed it out, and left that and the mug in the sink. Let her wash the damn thing whenever she got around to it. I looked around the counter for some paper towels, couldn't find them, then, out of habit, looked in the cabinet under the sink where I keep my own. I spotted a roll of Bounty behind a can of Comet and a bottle of Fantastic. But as I reached for it, I tipped over a wooden box shaped like a coffin that was pushed to the back of the cabinet.

It took me a minute to get it, to fully understand what lay on the kitchen floor before me: fountain pens, blood-red ink, Seconals. And, neatly tied with a purple ribbon, those hateful letters she'd written to Celia Jones. My body tightened with fear, as if what I'd found could reach out and strike me dead, too. I stood up slowly, then made my way back to the living room and my Kenya bag where I'd tucked that .38.

*S*he rocked back and forth in her dead husband's chair, and the creak of that chair and the howling wind outside seemed like the only sounds in the world. I looked for my bag, but it wasn't on the floor where it had fallen. It was beside her chair, as if it belonged to her. I knew then that my gun was in her hand. She must have remembered that the paper towels were under the sink, that I was bound to find her wooden box when I searched for them. I'd found out her secret, and now she would have to do something about it.

"You know, don't you?" Her voice was tired and heavy, as if she were talking in her sleep.

"Know what?" I made my voice light and innocent.

She made a sound that could have been a laugh but it came from too deep inside her throat. "You know because you found the letters. You found the pills."

"Why did you do it?" I asked, even though I knew she wasn't going to tell me. "I can guess why you killed Annette. When Celia gave her your letters, she must have recognized your handwriting, the paper, the ink. An old friend like her would know something like that.

Annette told me she always heard from you on holidays, that you two never failed to get together. But you didn't call her on New Year's Day, did you? So it probably didn't take much for her to figure out that you might have killed Celia Jones. But why did you kill her?"

There was no light in her eyes when she looked at me.

"I will say that I thought you were a burglar," she said. "That I heard a sound, came downstairs and you were in my living room, going through my things, and I shot you. That's what I will tell them."

There was no logic to what she said, and I told her so. "Right, Rebecca. You're going to tell them that I broke into your house and you shot me with my own gun. That doesn't make any sense, does it? Give it to me. Before it's too late. Just give me my gun, and we can work this out together."

But we both knew there was no working anything out together. That the truth can be twisted half a dozen ways, and that it always belongs to the person left to tell it. Only one of us would be left to tell it.

She rose to face me, moving slowly like a tired, old woman, like my grandmother had the day my young uncle was killed, as if all the light had gone from her life. The light was gone from Rebecca's life, too. She was as dead as her husband and baby, and I felt sorry for her. But not sorry enough to end up like Celia and Annette.

"He told me what happened between them, and he said it meant nothing, but he must have caught it from her, and so she killed my children, the children I should have had, and she wouldn't let me have the one she carried." I remembered what Laura Hunter had told me in the Biscuit about the judge's wife and the pelvic infection that might have rendered her sterile. Infections like hers could come from an IUD, but they could also be caused by a venereal disease like gonorrhea, I knew that, too. So she thought her husband had caught a disease from Celia and infected her, "killing her children," and Annette must have told her what she'd told me, that Celia was pregnant.

Never argue with a woman holding a gun. The best you can do is piece together what you know about the situation and try to figure out what to do about it. You can agree with her, too. Play back what she told you in your own words, and that's what I did.

"Yeah, Rebecca. I can certainly understand what you're saying. You were right. She took away your babies. It wasn't his fault though, it was all on her because she wouldn't let you have her child, right?"

She nodded like a kid, grateful that I understood her point.

"I went to her that day, to Celia Jones, because it was the first day of the year. Annette had told me she was pregnant, and that it could be anybody's child, and I thought it might be Clayton's. He said he hadn't had anything else to do with her, but I thought maybe he didn't know. Maybe it was something left of him. Maybe she would let me raise it because I didn't have anything else. But she laughed in my face and told me there was no baby. But I know she was lying because Annette told me there was."

And was that when you shot her through her womb? I thought.

"Celia Jones always was a liar," I said, edging closer to the door, wondering if she would shoot me before I could make a run for it. Then I remembered I didn't have my car keys; they were in my bag. "I can see how hurt you must have been, Becky," I said, my voice kind and sympathetic. "To go there on that morning to ask her to give you the baby, and she said she wasn't even pregnant. What a liar that woman was." I shook my head in agreement, then thought maybe I should go in another direction, wondered if there was something I could say that would shock her enough to throw her off, catch her off guard so I could make a lunge for the gun. I was stronger than she was, and I knew how to fight.

So I changed midstream, making my voice wheedling and nasty.

"But you did know that your loving husband, the late great Clayton Donovan, knew her before you introduced them, didn't you?"

She looked at me blankly, wondering what I was up to, not sure how to react.

I smiled as if caught in some pleasant memory. "I remember them in high school, Clay and Celia. They were lovers then, did you know that? Did you know that your husband, the late great Clayton Donovan, was the first man she ever slept with, she told me so herself. She told me before you killed her that he was going to leave you, and they were going to go off together. Isn't that why you really killed her, Becky?"

"No!"

I smiled knowingly and went on. "They say you never forget the first man you have sex with, and Clayton was her first. Did you know that, Rebecca? That's why he was giving her money before he died. How stupid could you be, Rebecca. So they were going to run off together and raise their child together."

It was coming off the top of my head, but there was just enough truth to make it sound convincing. I was sure now that Clayton Donovan was the *him* that Dawson had told me about yesterday. He was a big man with lots of respect who people admired. He hadn't been able to do anything else for her because he had died. I was sure he'd broken it off, like he'd told his wife. Men like him don't leave a prissy, high-class wife for a Celia Jones, but she obviously didn't know that.

"Your Clayton had been seeing her off and on for years. That was the real reason he'd made sure Brent Liston spent all that time in jail." I baited her, wondering what impact my words were having, but she just cocked her head to the side like a dog waiting to hear a master's whistle.

"He told me the truth before he died."

"The truth about Celia?"

"The truth that he had been seeing her. He asked me to forgive him. He begged me to forgive him. But I caught it from her nasty, diseased thing."

She was such a lady she couldn't bring herself to say the word she'd written in those letters. She sure could kill the girl, though, empty her gun into her "nasty, diseased thing."

"How do you know he caught it from Celia?" I grinned, teasing her. She looked at me strangely, cocking her head to the side again.

"Because she was a whore."

"Thou shalt not kill, Rebecca. You're a religious woman. How could you forget that?"

"She deserved to die for what she did to people who cared for her. Because she should feel God's wrath come down on her, and I could finally have some peace at last."

You need to find some kind of final resolution, one that will give you peace at last.

She had said those words to me before. How could I have missed the meaning behind them?

"Did killing Annette bring you peace as well?" She gazed at me, as if she didn't know what I was talking about, and I trotted out the theory I had about the way I thought Drew Sampson had done it, spitting it out with utter conviction, as if I'd been sitting in the room. "So you came by on Thursday morning, and she offered you a drink because she liked to drink, and you knew that she would. You sent her back for something, anything that took her out of the room, and then you put the Seconals you'd mixed with some of your husband's liquor into her drink. Enough to send her into a coma, and you two sat talking about old times until she began to get dizzy, and here's what you said to her when it started to take effect. 'Why don't you lie down, Annette? You might feel better. Let me put this pillow under your head, Annette, to make you comfortable. Try to go to sleep, Annette, and you'll feel better in the morning.' " I spoke in a high falsetto imitating a phony woman's voice, and she watched me, her gun steady on me as I continued.

"After she was out, you searched for the letters you knew she had because she had asked you about them, and before you left, you took her limp hand and made sure her fingerprints were on the gun, then put the gun and the drawing under her pillow."

"How did you know?" she said in her small, tight voice.

I edged toward the pedestal near the chair, close to the urn with her husband's ashes. The light from the fire, rather than the sun's rays, drew my attention to the golden lid this time.

"You know something, Rebecca? There were half a dozen women your husband could have caught it from. Hell, he even made a drunken pass at me, at a party a couple years ago. I knew he was a tramp, your late great Honorable Clayton Donovan, so I turned him down. He was one of the biggest cock hounds in the city. You talk about Celia being a whore. He was nothing but a whore, and he betrayed you every time he left your side."

"No!" she said, and for a moment I thought I'd gone too far because she raised the gun slightly, narrowing her eyes. My heart jumped, and I cursed myself for pushing her.

And then the phone rang.

Once. Twice. Three times. We stood transfixed, both of us. She turned to look at it, wondering who would know to call at that moment, who could have broken the spell between us, and that was when I made my move, turning fast in one quick motion, grabbing the urn from the pedestal, hurling it to the floor with all my might. The sound it made when it hit was as loud as her scream as she swooped down to gather what lay at her feet.

"Clayton!" It was a wounded moan like an animal makes when it's been shot. She fell down in the mix of broken china and her husband's ashes, dropping the gun to her side, and I went for it fast, nearly tripping over the man's remains as I dove for it.

"No!" she screamed as she grabbed for the gun, and we fell on the floor together, my head banging hard against the edge of the dead man's chair. She got the gun, grabbing it from my hand, and I pounced on her, surprised by the smooth silk against my arm. I pulled back my fist and whammed it hard into her jaw, and she moaned, dropping the gun again. I scrambled to get it, grabbed it, and struggled to my feet.

"He's gone," she whispered, with a look on her face I knew I would never forget.

"He's been gone."

"You took the last I had of him."

"Your choice, lady, not mine."

She stood up, and began to walk toward me. My heart jumped.

"Shoot me!" she said. "Please shoot me. I have nothing else to live for. Nothing else. Shoot me."

"Stop!" I stepped backward.

"Shoot me, damn you! I don't want to live anymore. Shoot me or I'll take that gun and shoot you and then myself. But I'll kill you first."

"Step back," I said.

She kept coming, her husband's ashes clinging like dust to her fancy black robe.

"Stop! Don't come any closer!" I didn't think I could shoot an unarmed woman; there was no way I could do it.

"Shoot me! Please, please shoot me!"

She was close enough now to get the gun. I took another step back, and she tried to grab it, her tiny hands grabbing and scratching my wrist.

And I thought about Celia lying there on that floor, her body filled with bullets, and Annette sipping that last drink with her trusted old friend. I thought about Jamal's laughter as we drove fast down the Parkway, about how much I loved him and how we were all each other had, and I knew at that moment that I'd be damned before I'd let this crazy woman make a motherless child out of my boy.

So I did what she asked.

When all was said and done—after the cops had gone, Rebecca's story told, and I was at home with my son—Jake dropped by to make sure I was all right.

"I really feel bad about the last time I saw you," he said, as I poured the champagne he'd brought to celebrate my solving the case.

"You mean last week with what's her name?" I asked, and he smiled without comment. We laughed easily then, like we always did, and I wondered, not for the first time, if I should share my true feelings.

But something had changed between us, and I didn't know if we could get it back. I didn't want Jake to leave my life, but if he did there was no way to stop him. I could only hope he'd return. If you hold too tightly to your past, you'll destroy your future. That was one good lesson I learned from Rebecca Donovan.

Larry Walton called after Jake left. He'd heard about what happened, and realized his call to Rebecca that day may have saved my life. I thanked him for it, and when he asked me out, I said I'd go.

Who knew what could come of it? A good meal, perhaps, and friendship if we were lucky.

I put Celia's locket in the place where I keep my precious things: Johnny's cuff links, Jamal's first gift, the paper dolls my grandma cut from newspaper.

"Catch you later, girl," I whispered as I closed the drawer.

And I slept well that night, like a baby in her papa's arms. My son was safe, I had *two* good men who cared, a new car that was running fine, and I'd caught the person who murdered my "used-to-be-best-friend." At least for now, all was right with the world.

Valerie Wilson Wesley has authored seven
Tamara Hayle mysteries and the novels *Always True
to You in My Fashion* and *Ain't Nobody's Business If I
Do,* for which she received the 2000 award for
excellence in adult fiction from the Black Caucus of
the American Library Association (BCALA).
All her novels have been Blackboard bestsellers and
When Death Comes Stealing was nominated for a
Shamus Award.

Ms. Wesley is also the author of several
children's books. She is formerly the executive
editor of *Essence* magazine. Ms. Wesley's fiction and
nonfiction for both adults and children have
appeared in many publications, including *Essence,
Family Circle, TV Guide, Ms., Creative Classroom,
The New York Times,* and *Weltwoche,* a Swiss weekly
newspaper. She is also a 1993 recipient of the Griot
Award from the New York chapter of the National
Association of Black Journalists. Ms. Wesley is a
graduate of Howard University and has master's
degrees from both the Banks Street College of
Education and the Columbia Graduate School of
Journalism. She is married to noted screenwriter
and playwright Richard Wesley and is the mother
of two grown daughters.

Whren
Robert James

Tue Aug 01 2017

Dying in the dark : a Tamara Hayle
mystery / by Valerie Wilson Wesley

31152064663638

p23166009

The End of 2017

Robert James
Warren